ANNIKA—A CHRISTMAS ROMANCE

ROSE MARIE MEUWISSEN

Annika—A Christmas Romance

By Rose Marie Meuwissen

Annika—A Christmas Romance

Digital/Print Edition

ISBN 978-0-9903788-4-6

Published in the United States of America

Nordic Publishing

Edited by Leanore Elliot

Cover Design by Angela Speed

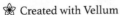 Created with Vellum

INTRODUCTION

Spend the holidays with Josie, Ryley, Emma, Alana, and Annika. Get ready for five weeks of romance with a new Christmas series brought to you by five exciting contemporary authors...

Betting on Paris!

Five exciting stories linked by a unifying theme. You'll want to read each one!

BETTING ON PARIS SERIES

Sometimes the best bet is the one you lose...

Five best friends. Five promises.

Each year in mid-August, the former college roommates meet up on a girls-only trip somewhere in the world. This year, it's Paris, the city of museums, art and romance. On the last night of their vacation, the girls engage in a serious talk about the sorry state of their love lives and collectively decide they are swearing off men. Instead, each woman is intent on pursuing her life's goal. Falling in love is the *last* thing on her mind!

This is *Annika's* story...

Owning Nordic Travel and Tours was a dream come true and Annika certainly didn't have time for romance. So why had she met the man of her dreams, now?

Tristan's Minnesota Events and Adventures Company for singles allowed him the ability to meet available women on a regular basis, so why would he be interested in her?

Annika had never mixed business with pleasure before and since Tristan would be booking tours through her company, there would be no romance. Now, she only had to convince her heart.

Find all the Betting on Paris novellas at Amazon!

Josie by Beth Gildersleeve
  Ryley by Donna Lovitz
  Emma by Angie Wilder
  Alana by Denise Devine
  Annika by Rose Marie Meuwissen

To my mom for taking me to Norwegian events, starting with Norway Day at Minnehaha Falls in Minneapolis when I was only 2 years old and for teaching me the Norwegian traditions from my father's home country, Norway, even though she was 100% German. The only German traditional food she ever mentioned was potato pancakes which I included in this story. Thank you, Mom, for all the wonderful memories and traditions!

1

After driving around the parking ramp for what seemed like an eternity, Annika pulled her SUV into an empty spot and quickly unloaded two medium-sized plastic tubs onto her wheeled cart, then hurried toward the glassed-in elevator. Plopping her purse down on top of the tubs, she pressed the button for the main level while her eyes focused on her phone to check the time. *Only thirty minutes until the doors open for the Minneapolis Travel Expo at the convention center.*

She took a couple of calming breaths, trying to erase visions of the backed up freeway she'd just spent way too much time on during the morning rush hour traffic. Thank God, she lived and worked in the suburbs! Absolutely no way, would she put herself through that rat race every day to get to work. The door opened and she backed out of the elevator pulling the cart with her, but stopped abruptly when she felt a firm pressure on her back. The top bin went crashing to the floor sending her travel brochures into a very messy pile beside her cart. She turned around quickly to see what had stopped her dead in her tracks.

Piercing blue eyes and sandy blond hair focused on her.

Her face flushed in embarrassment. "I'm so sorry. I'm in a hurry and wasn't watching what or who was behind me as I backed out of the elevator."

He grinned at her, sliding his phone into his pocket and bent down to retrieve a handful of brochures. "I can't let you take all the blame. I was on my phone and not paying attention to my surroundings, either. Let me help you." He picked up more of the fallen brochures and placed them into the plastic container.

Annika picked up the remaining brochures setting them in the bin, carefully placing the cover over the top, pressing down until she heard the click signifying it was on tightly. "Thank you. I do have to run though." She turned and quickly walked into the main ballroom with her cart in tow after flashing the security guard her exhibitor nametag.

Thankfully, the booth had already been set up last night by her assistant, Holly, who would be arriving around noon after her prenatal doctor's appointment. Annika hadn't a clue what she would do without Holly for three months, maybe more, while she was out on maternity leave. The baby was due in October which was coming up way too soon.

They'd been late getting the newly designed brochures to the printer, only being able to pick them up yesterday afternoon which was why she'd been hauling them into the Expo this morning. She neatly arranged them on the table, and then sat down on the comfortably padded chair to reign in her emotions after her collision in the hallway. Typically, she didn't do things like that, but today she was off her normal routine after dealing with the traffic and rushing to get into the Expo before the event started and the doors opened. Well, she'd made it with a few minutes to spare. She picked up a bottle of water, left at the table for them by the Expo, and downed almost half of it, wanting to stay hydrated since she was about to do a lot of talking to potential customers and clients.

The guy she'd bumped into was definitely good looking, but she'd sworn off men for a year to concentrate on her business. Recently, on a trip to Paris with her best friends, Alana, Josie, Ryley and Emma, they'd all made a pact to focus on their jobs and to not let *any* men interfere with their career plans for a year. *Betting on Paris—No Men for a Year* was their pact slogan. Besides, her dream of owning her own travel tour company, Nordic Travel and Tours, had come true after the first of the year, when her boss, Dan Nystad, retired and sold it to her. Dan felt she was the best person to run the company and take it to the next step into the tech future of the twenty first century. He'd been a friend and mentor, teaching her everything about travel and tours for the past ten years of her career. She needed no distractions this year, especially, to make all the transitions needed to take her company into the new tech age, for which, it was sorely lacking.

At nine o'clock on the dot, the Expo's doors opened and people rushed in, eager to find all the freebies like pens, hats and bags, but hopefully there would be many who wanted to book tours and were serious about traveling in Minnesota and other places in the world, like Scandinavia, which was her specialty. Her booth would be giving away pens and brochures imprinted with photos of exciting cities and places to visit.

Soon, the aisles were full of people and many stopped at her booth to gaze at the breathtaking photos of the fjords of Norway on the promotional banners. Nothing could match their beauty. She handed out brochures and answered questions, trying to remember to take sips of water in between potential clients.

Holly arrived at noon carrying what appeared to be her lunch along with a large purse filled with necessities for the long day. "I made it." Holly sat down on the chair.

"I hope you didn't have to walk very far."

"No, I got a spot in the parking ramp, but at seven months pregnant any walking takes extra effort."

"Go ahead and eat your lunch and when you're done, I'll go get something from the food vendors."

Annika continued talking with the people walking through the Expo until Holly finished eating.

Holly stood up and walked to the counter. "I'm done so go ahead and get some lunch. Bet you didn't have any breakfast and are starving." She shooed Annika out of the booth.

Tristan watched the woman walk away. She definitely had poise and class, and appeared to be very professional. *Extremely attractive, too.* He was intrigued, but this was a work day and he was on a mission today. His Minnesota Events and Adventures Company, for singles seeking new friends and adventure in the Midwest and abroad, needed a tour company. Leisurely, he made his way toward the coffee kiosk, since the doors wouldn't open for another twenty minutes. He felt confident in finding the perfect tour company for his company's travel needs today, if his gut feeling was accurate and it usually was.

Finally, when the doors opened for the Expo, Tristan walked up to the counter and greeted Holly. "Hi, I think this might be exactly what I'm looking for." He picked up a brochure which oddly looked familiar.

"Well, that would make my job easier." Holly laughed. "What can Nordic Travel and Tours do for you and your company?"

"My company is Minnesota Events and Adventures for singles. We set up events and travel destinations for our members. I'm looking for a company that can set up the tours and travel parts for us to sell as a group package to our clients. Basically, my company gets the people and your company would set everything up."

"This could be a perfect match because what we do is all the planning for trips such as the air, hotels, transportation and tours."

Tristan picked up a business card from the counter. "Are you Annika?"

"No, I'm Holly. Annika Karlstad is the owner and manager of the company and I'm her assistant." She pulled out her IPad with Annika's calendar. "I think you'd probably like to talk to her in person, so she can go over everything in detail. I have her calendar up on my IPad, so I'd be happy to set up an appointment next week for you."

Tristan pulled out his phone from his pocket and brought up his calendar. "Would Tuesday work?"

"She has a ten o'clock slot open."

"That should work." He pulled out his business card and handed it to Holly. "My name is Tristan Torgersen and I look forward to meeting Ms. Karlstad."

Holly smiled as she watched Tristan move on down the aisle past the rows of vendors.

Annika regretted not bringing a lunch when she saw the prices and the menu. Not that she had much choice at this point, so she ordered a salad and ice tea. While she waited for her food she checked her phone for any messages.

"So we meet again."

She turned to see who spoke. It was the man she'd literally run into earlier. "Hello. Again."

"How is the rest of your day going?"

"Much better. How about you?" Annika asked.

"Already made it half way through the auditorium. I think I've already found what I was looking for though."

"Oh, so will you still walk through the other half?"

"I'm here, so might as well take a look in case some other company strikes my fancy." Tristan chuckled.

"Well, best of luck...I guess I never got your name."

"Tristan."

"Well then Tristan, I'm Annika. Hope you find what you're looking for at the Travel Expo."

"I think I already may have found exactly what I'm looking for, Annika." Tristan smiled.

Annika heard her number called. "That's me. It's been nice running into you again." She gave him her best smile, then walked up to the counter to pick up her food. Discreetly, she positioned herself, so she could see if he'd left.

Tristan caught her eyes drifting his direction and tipped his head slightly in a nod, turned and walked back into the auditorium.

Why she felt so flustered around this guy, she had no idea. Her heart was racing and she knew she wanted to see him again. She knew nothing about him, so it was utterly ridiculous to be feeling this way. Besides, she wasn't looking for someone to date. At least not this year anyway, because she needed to stay focused on her company. She was personally responsible for making it a success. She didn't need any distractions.

After she'd finished eating her lunch, she made her way down a couple of aisles to check out the competition before going back to her booth. She felt confident about her company and what they had to offer clients. They offered bus tours to events and destinations in Minnesota and even some to the neighboring states of Wisconsin, Iowa, South Dakota and North Dakota. The tours to Scandinavia had always been top rated by their customers because they were unique in offering many off the beaten path options which were sought after by those with Scandinavian ancestry.

"Did I miss anything?" Annika asked taking a seat next to Holly.

"I put a couple of appointments on your calendar for next week that I think might be great new clients and handed out quite a few of the brochures."

"Tell me about the appointments."

"One is for a company looking to book some flight packages for their sales people who made their goals. And one is for the local company, Minnesota Events and Adventures. The company is for singles and they book group travel in and out of Minnesota for their events."

"Good job, Holly. Those sound like they have great potential for us."

A group of young people walked up to the table to ask about the trips to Iceland. Annika eagerly became engaged in conversation revolving around her passion for travel to the Scandinavian countries.

2

L ater the same afternoon, Tristan walked into his office at Minnesota Events and Adventures.

His sister, Britt Torgersen, immediately walked in after him.

"Hello, Britt."

"So how was it? Did you find us a tour company?" she asked.

"I think I might have. We'll know on Tuesday after I meet with their owner, Annika Karlstad."

"Okay... so you think they are the one? Are they big enough to handle all of our tours?"

"Shouldn't be a problem and Minnesota and Scandinavia are their specialties."

"Great! Hopefully, this will work out because we are behind schedule on getting these packages booked. And time is money in this business. The closer we get to the departure dates, the more money it will cost our members."

"I know, Britt. Trust me, I know. Anything else going on while I was gone today?"

"Matt Soderberg from Minnesota Events Magazine stopped by to see you. Why does that name ring a bell? He said he knew you."

"Yes. It's been a long time. We were friends in college. Didn't know he landed here in Minneapolis. What did he want?"

"He wants to go on one of our trips and maybe attend a couple of events so he can possibly write a cover story on our company. He made a point of letting me know he's single. This could be great advertising for us."

"Maybe, maybe not. You probably don't remember him since you were still in high school back then. Remember when I was engaged to Tonya after college and we'd already started planning the wedding?"

"Vaguely remember, but no one really told me much about the details."

"He's the reason the wedding was cancelled."

"Now, I remember Mother saying something about Tonya and another guy."

"Yes, she was cheating on me with Matt."

"Oh...that will make this rather difficult then..."

"Exactly. I've always wanted to be able to take a swing at him and you know I'm not that kind of guy."

"Okay, I'll just cancel the appointment I made for you two to talk. We don't need the publicity anyway."

"No, you can't do that."

"Sure, I can. I made the appointment, I can cancel it."

"No, he might retaliate and write something nasty about us just to get back at me."

"Wow, this sounds like a longstanding feud between you two. Are you still mad at him? I've met Tonya and you two wouldn't have made a good couple. He probably did you a favor."

"Probably, but it sure didn't feel like it at the time."

"How come he didn't marry her? Or did he? I mean he said he was single."

"After I called off the wedding, they broke up a few months later, then she left town and moved to Dallas. Never heard from her again. Or him. He left and moved to Chicago. Had no idea he was back in Minneapolis."

"I'm trying to remember what was going on back then. What was it ten years ago? Weren't you and Matt friends when you were attending UMD in Duluth?"

"You know I've never talked about this with anyone. Not sure why I'm sharing this with you now. But yes, we were best friends, college roommates."

"Tristan, I'm so sorry, I had no idea. I'll cancel the meeting."

"No. It's time I deal with this and face to face is probably the best way. Besides, he could apply to join our group anyway. If we declined him, it could get nasty. After all, he is a writer."

"Okay, then. The meeting is on Tuesday though, so I'll change it to Wednesday."

"That'll work. Let me know when you confirm a new date and time."

"Got it." Britt walked out the door closing it behind her.

Damn! He never wanted to see Matt again. There was no way he would ever trust him which was the main reason he didn't want to be around him. Although, he did feel a bit curious why it hadn't worked out with Matt and Tonya. He'd really thought they would've ended up getting married.

Annika was bone tired when she left the convention center that evening. It had been a successful day though. They'd gathered phone numbers and emails from more prospective customers than she'd expected. She felt happy with their first day at the convention. Since Nordic Travel and Tours had never participated in the local Travel Expo before, she hadn't known what to expect.

She was thankful the Expo ended after rush hour, as the cars on the freeway were now moving along nicely at the posted speed limit and some slightly over the speed limit. Tomorrow would be another long day, but she was looking forward to greeting more potential travelers for her company.

The one thing bothering her tonight was the crazy *Betting on Paris*

—*No Men for a Year* pact she'd made in Paris with her friends. Would they all take it seriously? If she went on a date, would that be against the rules? Probably. But what if she ran in to Tristan again and he asked her out for a drink? Was having a drink with a guy considered a date? Well, not technically. She'd met her fill of Mr. Wrongs and she wasn't about to pass on a chance of meeting Mr. Right. Deciphering men on first dates was something she was good at, she could tell the players and liars pretty quickly. For some reason, she felt a strong desire to go out with Tristan, but she had no idea why.

Most likely, it wasn't going to be an issue, though. She didn't know his last name and she hadn't given hers to him either, nor had they exchanged business cards. If he didn't happen to be at the Expo tomorrow, they would probably never meet again. So, this just wasn't going to be a problem and what she needed to do was stop thinking about him.

Saturday proved to be an even busier day, since it was a day off for most people. She chatted with people all day about the tours her company offered, all the while scanning the crowds for Tristan. *Why was she looking for him?* The day ended with no sign of Tristan. She came to the realization she would never see him again. Oh well, at least this way she could keep her word and honor the pact of swearing off men for a year.

3

Annika spent all day Monday going over the sign-up sheets from the potential customers from the Travel Expo. She'd put together a letter highlighting their upcoming tours and inviting them to a special event at her office to preview the tours and sit down one on one with her travel agents. The date for this event was next week on Thursday night. They needed to get these prospective travelers in quickly, so the tours could be booked for the upcoming months.

The next day, she had her appointment with Mr. Torgersen, the owner of Minnesota Events and Adventures, at ten. She was looking forward to talking to him about doing business with his company. She'd checked out his website and saw they did a minimum of ten tours a month. Some in Minnesota and the Midwest, and others abroad. This could be a golden ticket for her travel company. An alliance with them would boost her sales astronomically.

Tuesday morning, she took special care with her clothes and make up, picking a dark brown business suit with matching brown heels, and added a fall colored scarf she tied and let hang softly over the jacket lapels. Her blonde hair fell in gentle curls past her shoulders. She wanted to do business with *Minnesota Events and Adventures* more than she cared to admit. Her head held high knowing she could do this, she left the condo and drove to her office only ten minutes away.

"Holly, how are you feeling this morning?" Annika asked as she walked through Nordic Travel and Tour's front door.

"No issues today. How about you?"

"I'm doing great. Big day today."

"You look fabulous, today. You've got this." Holly beamed.

Annika walked into her office and sat down. She powered up her computer to look over any new emails. Then she prepared her folder for the meeting with Mr. Torgersen.

Tristan had looked forward to meeting Annika Karlstad. He was pretty sure she was the same woman who he'd bumped into by the elevator and talked to at the food window at the Travel Expo. She'd told him her name was Annika and he remembered seeing the picture of a Norwegian fjord on the back of the brochures that had fallen to the floor when they collided in front of the elevators. He'd told her his name was Tristan so he expected she knew he was the one she had an appointment with today.

Tristan Torgersen walked into Nordic Travel and Tours about ten minutes early for his ten o'clock meeting. "Good morning, Holly. I'm here to meet with Annika."

"Yes. If you'll just have a seat, I'll let her know you're here." Holly got up and walked down the hall to Annika's office.

"Mr. Torgersen is here."

"Please show him to the conference room. I'll be there in a couple minutes." Annika said a quick prayer this meeting went well and proceeded to shut down her laptop to bring with her into the conference room.

Holly walked back to her desk in the reception area. "Let me take you to the conference room and Annika will be with us shortly."

Tristan followed her down the hall and took a seat at the table.

Holly turned on a video promoting their tours. "I'll run this so you can get an idea of what we offer while you wait."

Tristan nodded and turned his attention to the screen. Five minutes later, Annika walked into the room. He turned his chair to face her.

Annika almost stopped dead in her tracks. It was him. *How could this be?* Quickly, she regained her composure, although she was sure he'd seen her shock at seeing him again. "Mr. Torgersen, so nice to meet you." She extended her hand to shake his.

He stood to greet her. "You can call me, Tristan. Always felt my dad was Mr. Torgersen." He held her hand a bit too long, before he sat back down.

She sat down and couldn't help staring at him as she was completely at a loss of words.

"I see you weren't expecting me from the look on your face." Tristan grinned.

"No, I wasn't."

"I was hoping it was you. I picked up a business card at your booth and it had your name on it. Annika is not a common name, so when you told me it was your name, I kind of figured you were with Nordic Travel and Tours, but I wasn't positive."

"I see. Holly had the appointment under Mr. Torgersen, so I had no idea it was you."

"Not a problem. Although, I have to say it's good to see you again."

"Tell me about your company and its travel needs." Annika sat down in a chair at the end of the table.

"Basically, my company offers singles in the Metro area an opportunity to attend events and to travel with groups of other singles. Although, we don't guarantee anyone will meet their special someone, it does happen quite often."

"How many members do you have?" Annika asked.

"Around a thousand."

"Okay, and how many trips do you plan per year?" she asked.

"Usually, two international trips and we typically plan at least one out of town trip per month to a unique event like a festival in a Minnesota town or a neighboring state. Also, sports events such as skiing, biking, snowmobiling, fishing and many others."

"Were you able to look at the tour brochures to see which tours you might be interested in for your company?"

"Yes. Lately, we've had quite a few retiree singles and they've expressed interest in Scandinavian events. I saw you have a trip to some event called 'Hostfest' in Minot, North Dakota at the end of the month. I know it's short notice, but I thought if you have any empty seats left on that motor coach, I'd like to offer them to my members."

Annika powered up her laptop and signed in to pull up the final counts on the Hostfest tour. "It looks like we had a group of fifteen cancel. The tour was sold out, but now we have these seats available. So if you'd like to offer them to your group, go ahead. I have to let you know I can only give you seven days and then I'll have to open it up to my staff to sell them so we can fill the seats. To be honest, it's usually tough to sell them at the last minute."

"Not a problem. I'll see what I can do." Tristan took out his phone and sent a text.

"I'll be traveling with this tour to Hostfest, so I'll be sure to take good care of your members," Annika said.

"I'm also interested in offering a ski trip to Lutsen in December. Probably early in the month."

"We have one already set for the week after Christmas, but let me see what I can do."

"Even if it is the week before Christmas," Tristan stated. "It might work since my members are single and may be available then. Many have expressed a desire to have an event to attend during the holidays since they don't usually have anywhere to go on those days."

"I'll check on it. About how many people would you have attending the ski event?"

"Let's shoot for between fifty and one hundred." He nodded. "Next year, I'd like to offer a winter break to someplace warm, probably somewhere in Europe for the summer, and a fall colors bus tour in Northern Minnesota. Maybe Duluth."

"We do offer some Mexico packages and if Scandinavia qualifies for your Europe tour package, I can help you with that. We always offer a fall color bus tour to both Duluth and Lake Pepin."

"It looks like we will be doing business together, then," Tristan said and smiled.

"I will put together all the info you need to sell the Minot tour. I'm going to get started working on the Lutsen ski trip right away. I'll let you know as soon as I secure hotel rooms and a bus. Once I get those confirmed, I can give you a per person cost."

"I'm looking forward to working with you, Annika," Tristan said rising from his chair to shake her hand.

Annika rose and extended her hand. "It looks like this union could be profitable for both companies." She motioned to the door and followed Tristan as he exited the room to walk down the hall leading to the reception lobby.

Tristan turned toward Annika and smiled. "I'll be waiting to hear from you."

"I'll contact you as soon as I get some firm numbers and confirmations on the hotels and buses."

Tristan nodded and left.

As soon as Tristan was out of sight, Annika walked back to her office and flopped down in her chair. She'd completely been caught off guard. She had no idea Tristan was going to be Mr. Torgersen. The man she felt super attracted to. *What is going on with me?* Of all times for her to meet a guy she was interested in dating. She'd just made a pact to swear off men for a year and Nordic Travel and Tours needed to be her sole focus right now.

"Are you all right?" Holly asked as she walked into the office.

"Not really, but I will be."

"I'm not following this. Do you want to fill me in on your meeting with Mr. Torgersen?"

"Well, let me tell you an interesting story, first. The day I picked up the brochures and brought them to the Travel Expo, I was in a hurry because I was running late due to all the traffic. I was pulling my mini cart loaded with the bins full of brochures. I backed straight into Tristan when I came out of the elevator. I was embarrassed to say the least. He helped me pick up the ones that fell and then I rushed into the Travel Expo."

"Oh, my." Holly sighed and sat down in a chair in front of Annika's desk.

"That's not all. After you arrived and ate your lunch, I went in search of something to eat. Well, I ran into Tristan again, or I should say he approached me. This time, he introduced himself as Tristan and I told him my name was Annika. Then my food was ready, so I left."

"So you knew it was going to be him you were meeting?"

"No. You told me I was meeting Mr. Torgersen. He never told me his last name."

"I'm so sorry, Annika. I had no idea."

"I know. But the real kicker is he had my business card, so he was pretty sure he was meeting me."

"He seemed like a nice enough guy," Holly interjected.

"Oh, he probably is."

"So, I'm not understanding. Then, what is the problem?"

"I'm just the unluckiest person when it comes to men."

"What?"

"I never told you this, but remember my trip to Paris with my friends, Alana, Josie, Ryley and Emma?"

"Yes, didn't you have a great time in Paris?"

"Oh, we had the best time there. But everyone was having so much trouble with men, so we decided to swear off men for a year. We made a pact and called it, *Betting on Paris—No Men for a Year.*"

"I don't understand."

"I don't have time for a guy in my life right now anyway, what with running Nordic Travel and Tours, so I figured I didn't care about some stupid bet anyway."

"And now you've changed your mind?"

"You saw him. Isn't he one of the best looking guys you've ever met?"

"Well, I'm a little partial to my husband, Tom, being one of the best looking guys I've met. But, yes, he is a handsome guy."

"Exactly, that's the problem with this whole situation. And even if it wasn't for the promise I made in Paris, I still couldn't even think about dating him. Not that he's asked, mind you."

"He did seem interested in you."

"Never mix business with pleasure. That's a promise I made to myself a long time ago."

"Looks like it's settled then. If he asks you out, the answer is no."

"Let's hope he doesn't ask and then my problems would be solved."

"If he wasn't a client and there wasn't a pact with your friends, then you'd go out with him?"

"Heck, yes."

"I see, then we just have to make sure he doesn't ask." The front door opened in the lobby. "I'll see who's here." She left the office.

Annika had thought it would make her feel better to discuss her feelings about Tristan with someone. Holly had been that lucky person. Sadly, it hadn't made her feel any better about the situation. The only thing she could do was act professional when dealing with him. Hopefully, they would be able to do all communications by phone or email. No more in person meetings. If she didn't have to see him, she wouldn't be tempted to accept any invitations from Tristan. That is, if he even offered any. Basically, she felt like she had made their meeting into much more than it really was.

4

The next day, Annika sent over the promo material via email for the fifteen available seats on the bus tour to Hostfest in Minot. She really didn't expect any of Tristan's members would be interested in this tour. Generally, it appealed mostly to the older retirees with Scandinavian backgrounds. Not as if there weren't any of those people in the Metro area, but she didn't think many of these people were members of his company. Maybe, she was wrong. She really didn't know much about his company or its members, but somehow she pictured them as being in their twenties to forties.

Attending Hostfest yearly was one of her favorite tours. A four day tour, leaving Minneapolis on Tuesday morning, spending three nights in a hotel, allowing them two full days at Hostfest and returning to Minneapolis on Friday. The event had always been held the last week of September and had a large following. Unfortunately, the attendees were aging. The regulars were in their late seventies and eighties, which meant they were dying on a regular basis. Attendance was down, and they were desperately trying to attract the younger generations which appeared to be a tough sell. Hopefully, the directors of the event would find a way, because it was a large all-encompassing celebration of Scandinavian heritage.

She gave Tristan a week to see if he could sell the open seats on the bus. Afterwards, she would put the seats out to her sales force to fill.

Next, she contacted her hotel reps in Lutsen, to see what they had available in December. She put a call in to the bus company to see what they could give her in December, as she needed both to put together a tour for Minnesota Events and Adventures. The other factor to be considered was the snow situation. Some years, nature provided snow and other years the ski hills did. Of course, Mother Nature's snow was always preferred. Generally, by December Lutsen had snow, though, so it shouldn't be a problem.

Her phone rang. "Nordic Travel and Tours, Annika speaking."

"It's Sandy from Lutsen lodging. I wanted to get back to you right away. The weekend before Christmas, we could hold thirty-five rooms. I know you were looking for thirty to fifty, but hopefully out of those numbers you should have some doubles."

"Thanks, Sandy. Thirty-five is great. When is your cut off for confirmation?"

"Let's say December 1."

"Okay, let me see what I can do to sell these rooms."

"We'll talk soon. Bye."

Annika quickly sent an email to Lutsen ski department to get a package price for ski rentals and lift tickets.

She checked her emails and saw a reply from the bus company. They could do the first weekend or the weekend before Christmas. This was perfect. She sent them back an email choosing the weekend before Christmas. This was working out better than she'd expected. She got up from her desk and walked down to the lobby. "Holly, I just sent you an email with all the info for Tristan's ski trip to Lutsen. The hotel and bus are confirmed along with a ski package. Please check with the hotel restaurant for a meal plan. Since it's so close to Christmas, see if they can offer snowmobile rides and maybe a special Christmas dinner. I want to get a promo brochure put together on this as soon as possible. Let Jason, our expert in marketing, know it will be coming his way soon."

"Great. Glad this is working out. Will you be escorting this one?"

"Well, I certainly don't expect you to be skiing shortly after having a baby." Annika and Holly both broke out laughing.

"Sorry, you will have to take this one, Annika."

"Not a problem. It'll be fun. You know I love all this Christmas stuff. It's kind of my thing."

"I know it's been hard since your parents retired and moved to Arizona."

"I'll book a flight to Phoenix for the day after I get back from Lutsen. At least, this way I'll have sort of a white Christmas, it'll just be a few days early."

Tristan received Annika's email regarding the Hostfest trip's promo. He immediately forwarded it to Britt to do her magic and sell the seats. She had strict orders to only sell fourteen, because he would be going on this particular tour.

Later the next day, he received another email from Annika with all the info on the Christmas ski package to Lutsen. She had a great graphic artist, because the brochure looked fabulous. It oozed with Christmas spirit and colors. Anyone would want to book this tour even those who didn't ski. He forwarded the email to Britt, also stating he would be going on the tour.

Britt walked into Tristan's office. She appeared to be in an agitated state. "I posted all the info for Hostfest on the website."

"Great!"

"Matt Soderberg just called to book a seat. He wants to write an article for the magazine."

"Damn!" He slammed his fist down on his desk.

"What should I do?"

"We don't have any choice but to go ahead and book him a seat."

"Do you still want to go?" Britt asked.

"Yes."

"Just saying, I'm not going. You're on your own on this one, brother." Britt left his office and headed to her office.

Tristan felt angrier than he'd been in a long time. He didn't trust Matt one little bit. Annika wouldn't be safe, in fact, he was sure Matt would consider her fair game. Once Tristan showed even one ounce of interest in her, the game would begin. Damn! He was interested and intrigued by her. She appeared to be a strong independent woman and the sexual chemistry between them was definitely there. He'd felt it every time he'd been near her. She'd seemed a bit nervous around him which he took for her interest in him. Sexually, that is. Now, he would need to tread lightly because as soon as he showed any interest in Annika, it would be a competition to Matt. And Matt didn't like to lose.

By the end of the week, Tristan received the brochure template for the Lutsen ski trip in December. He forwarded it to Britt to put on the website. He'd been pretty impressed by the package Annika had put together for his company. It was a four night package including the bus, hotel, meals, a ski or snowmobile package and a special Christmas dinner party for a very reasonable price. His people were going to love it. He was planning on having a very nice time in Lutsen with Annika. Hopefully, Matt would be long gone by then.

"Tristan, we now have all fifteen seats filled for Hostfest. Which includes you and Matt." Britt took a seat in front of his desk.

"Great. I'm looking forward to this trip."

"Really? Doesn't sound fun to me at all," she said.

"You do know our great-grandparents came from Norway?"

"Yes, I remember Mom always talking about them. I even remember her taking us to some event in the summer at Minnehaha Park. I think it was called Norway Day. Do they even celebrate it anymore?"

"I remember the event, too. Haven't heard it advertised anywhere recently. Maybe they quit having it."

"I always liked the lefse with the butter, cinnamon and sugar all rolled up inside it."

"I'm actually looking forward to trying the Nordic ethnic foods up at Hostfest."

"If Mom were still alive, she'd be proud of you. In fact, she probably would've insisted on going with you." Britt's eyes teared up as she thought about her mother.

Tristan stood up and walked around his desk to where Britt was seated. He gently rubbed her shoulders. "Dad wouldn't have cared in the least. He never supported Mom doing anything to do with her heritage, which is why we weren't brought up with the old traditions. This is one of the reasons I wanted to go on the tour."

Britt cried now. "If Dad hadn't been driving drunk, Mom would still be here and they wouldn't have died in the car accident. I miss her so much."

"I never understood why she didn't divorce him. He wasn't a good person. Everyone knew it, but she seemed oblivious to what kind of person he really was."

"I'm pretty sure she knew, but she didn't know how to walk away. By the time we'd both gone away to college, I think she was considering a divorce, but never got the chance because of the accident."

Tristan sat down in the chair next to Britt and took her hands in his. "Don't cry. We can't change any of that. I'm going to check out Hostfest this year and if it's as wonderful as they claim, we'll both go next year. I don't want you there this year because I don't want you to get mixed up in this whole mess with me and Matt."

"I know, you're right. I'm going to hold you to this. Next year, we're going together to Hostfest. I want to get there, before they stop holding the event, like Norway Day which may have already ended." Britt wiped her eyes and stood up. "I'm okay. I'll send Annika all the info for the members who signed up."

"Then on to the Lutsen ski trip. Let's get those seats sold," Tristan said and teased Britt as she walked out of his office.

5

Annika was surprised, to say the least, when later that week she received an email from Britt at Events and Adventures stating they'd sold all fifteen seats. She was impressed Tristan was able to pull it off with less than two weeks before the tour date. Before she knew it, she'd picked up her office phone and punched in his office phone number.

"Tristan speaking," he answered.

"This is Annika. I just wanted to congratulate you on selling those fifteen seats to Hostfest."

"I told you, my members would be interested."

"Well, yes you did. I'm looking forward to showing them a good time. It's an event I've enjoyed for the last ten years and still do."

"Good to hear, because I'm looking forward to the trip myself."

Annika almost dropped the phone. She should've put him on speaker phone. "You will be joining us?" she asked.

"Yes. It may surprise you to know I'm part Norwegian."

"Really." Annika felt both dread and anticipation roil through her body.

"This tour will give me a chance to experience my heritage."

"Great. I look forward to showing your group–including you–

what Scandinavian heritage is all about." She needed to end this call soon because she was treading on thin ice.

"We're working on selling the ski trip, as we speak. I want to commend you on putting together an excellent package and price. Will you be leading the trip?"

"Yes, since it was last minute, my other travel leaders are already booked."

"You made it look so enticing, I've decided to join the tour, also. Looks like we will be spending some time together in the upcoming months."

"Yes, it appears that way. I need to let you go now. I have a meeting in a few minutes."

"Bye, we'll be in touch."

"Bye," Annika said, hung up the phone and leaned back in her chair.

She was doomed. How was she supposed to act like she wasn't interested in him if they would be in constant contact for multiple days on both trips? There were promises she needed to keep both to herself and her friends. She didn't have time to waste feeling sorry for herself, so she stood up and went in search of Holly.

"Do we have everything set for Hostfest?" Annika asked.

"Yes, just confirmed with the hotel. Tickets for Hostfest will be waiting at the Will Call desk under your name. There will be separate tickets for the Celtic Woman concert performed on Thursday evening and the private dinner for the group at *En To Tre*–the six course taste of Scandinavia fine dining restaurant on Friday evening."

"Sounds like you have everything under control. Not sure what I'm going to do without you when you're on maternity leave."

"You'll be fine. I'm training in Becca, besides it will be our slow season anyway."

"I know. I just talked to Tristan and he is planning to join me on both the Hostfest tour and the ski trip."

"Oh, I'm so sorry. Although, I just have this gut feeling it will all work out for the best."

"Thanks. I guess it's probably the best attitude to have, since there aren't really any other options. I want to go on these two tours and so does he, apparently. I can only hope he doesn't turn out to be the perfect guy of my dreams."

A week later, Annika stood looking into her closet, trying to decide which clothes to bring to Hostfest. She pulled out two Norwegian sweaters and laid them on her bed along with jeans and a pair of dress pants. The weather forecast was for cooler weather in the forties and fifties. She selected a couple of Scandinavian designed jackets, her leather boots and continued packing the other necessities for her trip.

She couldn't believe the bus was leaving tomorrow morning at nine. Her excitement for the trip was drowning out her dread from being in close quarters with Tristan. All she could do was act professional and do her job.

The next morning, she hurried out to her SUV with her bags in tow. After she stopped to pick up a coffee in the drive thru, she drove to the Eden Prairie transit station where the bus would be waiting. There was plenty of parking for the tour passengers to leave their vehicles for the duration of the tour trip, so it was the perfect place to board the bus.

Holly was already there to hand out the trip packets which included parking passes to place inside their windshields. Annika spotted Tristan walking towards her. Quickly, she brought her suitcases to the bus driver to put under the bus. Then, she entered the bus to drop her bag on the front seat. As she stepped out of the bus, she saw Tristan waiting for her a few feet away from the door.

"Good morning, Ms. Karlstad," Tristan said with a grin and placed his suitcase under the bus.

"Good morning to you, Mr. Torgersen."

"I'd like to sit up front, if you don't mind." Tristan moved to stand directly in front of her.

"Sure." Annika waved her hand toward the steps.

He entered the bus and placed his bag on the seat across the aisle from where Annika apparently already had placed her bag on the seat, then exited the bus.

A man approached the table where Annika was greeting the passengers.

"Your name?" Annika asked.

"Matt Soderberg, writer for Minnesota Events Magazine. Really happy to be joining your tour to Hostfest. I'll be writing an article on your company and the festival."

"I wasn't aware you'd be joining us," Annika stated giving him the once over.

"I'm booked with the Events and Adventures group. Tristan and I are old college friends. I didn't catch your name," Matt stated coyly.

"Annika Karlstad. I'm the owner of Nordic Tours and Travel. Welcome to our Hostfest tour. I hope you enjoy it." She handed him his packet which included a seat assignment in the middle of the bus. "I wasn't aware you and Tristan were friends, if you'd like to sit together, I can see if I can move you?"

"That's not necessary, but if you can arrange a seat change, let me know." He picked up his packet and walked toward the bus to drop his bags.

Tristan briskly walked by Matt, only nodding his way. He headed toward Annika. He waited until she was available and then approached her.

She stood with her full five feet two height staring up into Tristan's baby blue eyes. He was tall just a little over six feet. "A little heads up about your friend joining us to write an article on the tour, would've been nice."

He smiled and took a step closer to Annika. "You're absolutely right, I apologize. Only recently did I find out he was back in town. We haven't kept in touch since college."

"Fine." Annika couldn't help taking in a large whiff of his cologne. He smelled awfully good. Oh and how his jeans hugged his body including a tapered shirt, spoke volumes about how he most likely worked out daily. His sandy blond hair appeared sophisticatedly styled. *What am I doing?* She cleared her throat and backed away. *How had he gotten so close to me?* "I have to go," she finally said and walked away.

Everyone was checked in and they boarded the bus fifteen minutes later. It wasn't until all the passengers were seated and they were on their way to Minot, North Dakota, a mere ten hour drive, when she finally thought about Matt. She'd forgotten to try and change his seat. Oh well, it was too late now. Thankfully, the young man seated behind Tristan had engaged him in conversation so he hadn't tried to strike up a conversation with her. Yet. She hadn't slept well last night, so it wasn't a wonder she quickly dozed off resting her head on the window beside her seat.

The bus would make a stop at a rest area every two hours. As soon as the bus parked, she woke up. After everyone exited the bus, including Tristan, she stood up and stepped onto the asphalt. She was glad to make conversation with two older ladies after her stop in the restroom. Soon, they were on their way again.

Next, they stopped in Fargo for lunch at the West Acres Mall, where everyone was on their own in the food court. She ordered a sandwich and sat down at a table to eat with a couple of younger women who wanted to pick her brain about the best things to do at Hostfest.

Annika felt thankful Tristan kept his distance during the rest of the drive. The bus stopped in Bismarck for dinner at an established icon restaurant, Kroll's Diner, where they had a reservation for fifty people. A limited menu was offered so they could serve such a large number of customers in a timely manner.

Amazingly, they were back on the road again, an hour later. A little after nine, the motor coach pulled into the Minot Holiday Inn. Everyone was eager to gather their luggage, check in and retire for the evening.

Annika watched Matt leave the counter and disappear into the elevator.

Next, Tristan checked in and retrieved his room key card from the counter. Annika was the only one left. "I'll see you in the morning," he said, smiled broadly at her, then walked over to the elevator.

"Yes, it's been a long day." She turned back toward the desk clerk as he handed her a key card. When she turned toward the hall with bags in tow, she saw Tristan still waiting for the elevator.

"Guess you just can't get rid of me," Tristan said as the doors opened. He waited for her to enter the elevator first.

"I'm not trying to get rid of you. I'm just too tired to do any more conversing."

The doors opened and they exited the elevator on the fourth floor. She walked down the hall to 410, her room.

Tristan walked past her to the next room 412. "Looks like we're neighbors. See you in the morning. Breakfast at seven?" he asked.

"I'll probably still be sleeping and I'm skipping breakfast. I love the Norwegian heart shaped waffles they serve at Hostfest. They'll be my breakfast tomorrow. See you on the bus at nine." She didn't wait for a response while she opened the door and walked into her room.

"Goodnight," Tristan said.

The bus pulled out of the parking lot promptly at nine the next morning and everyone walked into Hostfest by nine-thirty. Annika walked over to the Will Call desk to get their tickets. The lady handed her an envelope with the badges for everyone on her tour. Inside the clear pockets of the badges were their entrance, dinner and concert tickets. After reminding everyone the bus would be leaving promptly after the evening concert at nine-thirty, they all headed off in different directions.

Annika knew the layout of Hostfest from her past visits and made her way immediately to the Nordic Waffle booth. She ordered her favorite butter, cinnamon and sugar waffle, then sat down to enjoy every delectable bite.

"There you are," Tristan said walking up beside her. "That looks interesting. I think I'll have to try one." After looking over the menu, he ordered the breakfast waffle filled with eggs, bacon, and cheese at the counter. Then he walked over to where Annika sat. "Care if I join you?"

"No, have a seat." *What am I supposed to say? I can't tell him no.*

He sat down next to her and took a bite of his waffle. "This is delicious. Is this a Nordic traditional food?"

"Yes. Well not so much with the filling inside yours, but the plain waffles are. Now they put all different things on them." She picked up her Hostfest schedule and looked over the entertainment times. It would be rude to just get up while he was eating, so she waited.

"Do you have a path through this maze of vendors you use each time or do you change it up?"

"I generally start by going to the right and making my way through all the wings then make my way back to the entrance and continue to the left side's hallways."

"Do you mind if I tag along with you?" he asked. "I really don't know too much about my Norwegian heritage and you seem to be somewhat of an expert on the subject."

What can I say to that? "Of course, feel free to join me. Just keep in mind, I'm a woman, and I'll be stopping to shop along the way."

"Got it. And thank you." He grinned at her and followed her down the closest aisle.

Around one in the afternoon, they worked their way back to the food court to try more of the ethnic foods for lunch. She opted for the Klub, a traditional Nordic food similar to a potato dumpling with a ham broth.

Tristan decided to try it, too.

Shortly after they sat down, Matt appeared. He set his lunch selection down on the table and snapped a couple pictures of Annika eating the Klub. "For the article," he said. Then he proceeded to sit down with them to eat his meatball on a stick.

"How's your day going?" she asked.

"This place is fantastic. Really loving all the Troll and Viking statues. Everything is quite Nordic. This meatball on a stick is pretty good, too. Do you think they got the 'on a stick' thing from the Minnesota State Fair?"

"Sounds like you're having a good time," Annika stated flashing Matt a bright smile. "Should we tell them about the long standing tradition of almost everything on a stick being a Minnesota tradition not a Nordic tradition?"

"I think we can let it slide." Matt laughed and finished eating quickly.

"I'm going to continue down to the North Halls. See you later at the concert." Annika got up and walked away.

"Leave her alone, Matt," Tristan said after he made sure Annika was out of hearing range.

"What's that supposed to mean?" Matt asked.

"You know exactly what I'm talking about. I know the games you like to play with women. I don't want her to get hurt."

"You wound me with your words, man."

"Don't even try to pretend you haven't set your sights on Annika. It's quite apparent you've decided to try your luck at getting her interested in you." Tristan stood up.

"The thought hadn't even entered my mind," Matt said as he finished eating and got up to leave, also.

"Stay away from her, Matt." Tristan walked off in search of Annika.

6

Annika walked out of the food hall, away from the unwanted temptation of Tristan and Matt. They both were blessed with looks which could easily land them on the cover of a GQ magazine. She definitely didn't need to be involved with a man, much less two men, at this point in her life. Maybe, she was just imagining that either of them was even interested in her. She needed to stay focused on her company's success and keeping her promise to her friends. Her luck hadn't been good in the past, as far as her love life went, and she didn't have the time to waste on a relationship that probably wouldn't work out anyway.

She walked into the Viking Hall and stopped to look at a booth featuring authentic replica Viking Era jewelry. Each year at Hostfest, she treated herself to a new piece of jewelry and this year her heart was set on a Viking piece. She picked up a sterling silver necklace with what appeared to be a white ball of glass wrapped in a silver pendant.

"This is a replica piece of a necklace found in a burial mound in Gotland, Sweden," the lady behind the counter explained. "Go ahead and try it on."

Annika fastened the necklace around her neck and looked into the mirror the woman held out for her. Staring back at her was a breathtaking beautiful necklace along with a very handsome man walking up behind her."

"I think you should get this one," Tristan said.

She turned around so abruptly that she stopped just as quickly, which was when she realized she was only inches from his firm chest. His lips were only inches from hers. Immediately, she turned back towards the mirror.

"I do think it may be exactly what I was looking for, I may have to buy this one."

He was making her extremely nervous by standing so close to her. She reached up behind her neck to unfasten it. She set it down on the counter gazing at it with longing. Casually, she flipped the tag over and saw the high price.

"I just got here so I'm going to think about it, I may be back." Annika walked away down the aisle and around the corner.

Tristan hesitated for a moment till she was out of sight. "I'll take it," he said to the lady still holding the necklace and handed her his credit card. After she handed him the necklace wrapped in a bag, he slipped it in his pocket and walked in the same direction as Annika.

"I thought I'd lost you." Annika stopped, seeing him approach her.

"Not a chance I'd give up my tour guide, just stopped along the way to look at something interesting."

"Well, try to keep up." She laughed.

They walked through two more halls, shopped, listened to some Ole and Lena jokes from a comedian performance on a stage, and finally stopped in another food hall to have dinner. This time, they opted for a salmon dinner.

Just as they were finishing, Matt approached them. "Wow, this is really a big place. Wasn't sure which way you'd gone, Annika. But figured you'd probably be in one of the food halls around this time."

"Did you have a nice afternoon?" Annika asked politely.

"Yes, ran into some of the other people from our tour. Great group of people you have who signed up for this tour, Tristan. And it included a very attractive tour director," Matt stated.

Annika felt uncomfortable upon hearing his compliment. "Would you care to join us?" she asked, not knowing what else to say.

"The salmon looks delicious. I think I'll get some and join you two in a few minutes." Matt walked over to the nearby counter to place his order.

"He seems like a nice guy," Annika said to Tristan.

"Can't vouch for that, it's been years since I've been around him."

"What does that mean?"

"Sometimes, people change and sometimes, they don't." He finished eating his meal.

A few minutes later, Matt joined them.

Tristan and Annika discussed the Nordic items that had caught their attention in the booths earlier that day, while Matt continued eating his meal.

When he'd finished, the threesome made their way to the concert hall. Annika took out her ticket to see which door she needed to enter. It didn't surprise her in the least when Tristan announced his seat was next to hers.

A somewhat defeated look crossed Matt's face when he realized his seat wasn't anywhere near Annika. "Enjoy the concert. I'll catch you both later." Matt walked away to find door G where his seat was located.

"Shall we?" Tristan said motioning toward door D.

Annika approached the door, handing her ticket to the person at the door to scan and walked into the concert auditorium.

Tristan followed her and they found their seats.

"This should be a great concert," she stated.

"I've never heard Celtic Woman's music before, but it sounds like you may have?"

"Yes. I even have a few of their CD's. I especially like the

Christmas one. They're really good. I think you'll be glad you came to hear them perform."

"Are they Scandinavian?"

"No. They're from Ireland. The group started in 2005 and have released somewhere around fourteen CDs. They perform concerts all over Europe and the U.S."

"Sounds like you're one of their fans," Tristan said while they waited for the show to begin.

"I have to admit I have *all* their CDs along with a few DVDs of their live concerts."

"Do you have a favorite song?"

"That would be, *Oh, America*. Every time I hear it sung by them, it brings tears to my eyes. It's so good."

"Will they sing it tonight?"

"We'll have to wait and see."

Soon, the lights dimmed and the Celtic Woman group took the stage backed by a full orchestra. The violinist, part of their group, came out in full force dancing while she played the violin as the crowd cheered.

Near the end of the concert, they announced the song, *Oh, America*. Annika became engrossed in the words and meaning of the song. This song always made its way into her heart and soul. The music was just that good. She couldn't help thinking about all the Norwegian immigrants who came to America with only one bag of meager belongings and hardly any money to find a better life. During those years of the late 1800's and early 1900's, they all passed through Ellis Island where the Statue of Liberty welcomed them all with open arms.

Half way through the song, her eyes teared up and she could feel Tristan's eyes on her, but she resisted looking his way. Instead, she focused on the singers.

There were a few more songs as the crowd stood and clapped after each one. At the closing, the Celtic ladies on stage joked about Ireland being added to the list of Scandinavian countries since many Vikings from Norway, Sweden and Denmark had settled in the Irish

Isles. At the least they suggested, maybe Ireland could become an *honorary* Scandinavian country. Everyone stood up clapping and cheering. Celtic Woman left the stage and the lights were raised.

"I thoroughly enjoyed the concert," Tristan stated with a smile. "And I think you're right, the *Oh, America* song was one of the best ones they performed. I think I may have to see if I can download a few of their songs to my phone."

Annika smiled. She liked him. It was almost like they'd been on a date. *Only they hadn't.* She followed him out to the hallway and they made their way to the front entrance along with the crowd of people exiting the concert. She'd forgotten about Matt until she saw him waiting outside the front entrance doors for their bus. He smiled her way. Could she avoid him? She'd had a great time with Tristan and wasn't ready for their *date* to end. *Well, it was kind of like a date.* Unfortunately, she watched as Matt approached them. Luckily, just as he made it over to where she and Tristan were standing, the bus pulled up.

"Hope you enjoyed the concert. Back to work for me." She pointed to the bus and took out a clipboard from her bag. She stepped in front of the door and started checking names off as they entered.

Reluctantly, Matt boarded the bus, while Tristan hung back to wait till she'd checked everyone off her list. He was the last one to board.

The ride back to the hotel was quiet since everyone seemed worn out from their full day at Hostfest. Once back at the hotel, everyone exited the bus and headed to their rooms.

Annika found herself in the lobby with both Matt and Tristan hanging back, apparently waiting for her. "See you two in the morning." She walked past them to the elevator, half expecting them to follow, but they didn't. The doors opened and she entered it alone.

Once in her room, she undressed and got ready for bed. To say, she was tired would be an understatement. She was completely exhausted. *What am I going to do about my growing feelings for Tristan?* He was off limits in more ways than one. If she were to choose between the two, Matt would be a better choice since he wasn't her client. But something about him made her feel leery. For some reason, he didn't seem sincere. Like something else was going on with him. Oh hell, she didn't know enough about either one to be making any judgements about their sincerity, especially since she wasn't in the market for a boyfriend. She crawled into bed and fell asleep in only minutes.

"How was your date with the hot tour lady?" Matt asked Tristan.

"It wasn't a date."

"Sure looked like one. Appears you're really interested in her. Is that why you wanted me to back off?"

"She doesn't deserve to be involved in one of your games."

"Awe, you wound me. Maybe I'm interested in her for real." Matt sneered.

"Not a chance in Hell. It's only the chase you're interested in," Tristan gritted out as his hands formed fists.

"Annika will be doing the choosing. Let the best man win." Matt laughed and walked away.

Tristan did feel intrigued by Annika. He had no doubts now. He definitely would be pursuing Annika. No way would he let Matt hurt her and he knew Matt would do it, if only out of spite. *Oh hell, let the games begin.* This was one game he intended to win, mainly so he could save Annika from Matt. A part of him knew he wanted to win because he actually wanted to have a relationship with her. It had been a long time since he'd let anyone near his heart, maybe it was time. What scared him the most was Matt could be clever and conniving when it came to a woman he desired. He'd witnessed it first-hand. There was every possibility Matt could win.

7

The next morning, Annika woke refreshed and ready to take on the day, along with Matt and Tristan. Not since college, had there been two men interested in her at the same time. She remembered it vividly and it hadn't turned out well. Unfortunately, she'd chosen badly and watched a good man walk away. Nick, the one she'd picked had dumped her shortly after their college graduation.

When she walked outside to check in with the bus driver, she spotted Matt chatting with a couple of ladies. He quickly looked her way, so she nodded and kept on walking. A few minutes later, she started the boarding process.

Matt had been watching from a distance and finally made his way over to the bus. "Good morning, Annika."

"Good morning, Matt." She checked his name off on her list.

"I'd like to interview you sometime today and ask you a few questions for my article, if that's okay with you?" Matt gave her his official heart stopping smile.

"Sure. I'm sure I can fit in a few minutes for an interview."

Matt nodded and boarded the bus.

Tristan watched the last person board, before he walked over to Annika. "Good morning, Annika. You look nice. I like your sweater."

"Good morning, Tristan. Thank you, I purchased this sweater yesterday."

"Maybe I should buy one today?"

"I'd be happy to help you pick one out. Are you ready for another day at the Hostfest?"

"Can't wait," he said and boarded the bus.

Annika stepped on after him. "We have everybody," she said to the driver and took her seat in the front row.

The bus driver shifted the gear and they were on their way.

Once they arrived at Hostfest, everyone dispersed quickly, except for Tristan and Matt. What was she supposed to do? Walking around with both of them would be difficult, especially since she sensed some sort of conflict between the two of them.

Abruptly, two of the ladies from Tristan's tour group walked back to the front door and up to Matt. She watched as they took him by the hands and pulled him along with them. Soon the three of them were laughing while exiting the front entrance area and heading down the hallway. Unconsciously, she let out a deep breath of relief.

"Well, that was close. Thought for a moment, I was going to have to share you with Matt, this morning," Tristan said after he moved nearer to Annika.

"Yes, it appears it will be just us this morning," she said smiling at him. "This way to the sweater shops."

Tristan followed her lead into one of the large halls. "Isn't this the food area? I thought you said we were going to buy a sweater?"

"We are, but first…"

"I see. Waffles. I'm up for sampling a different one this time for my breakfast. Lead the way."

Annika ordered her second favorite, Nutella and a bottle of water. Tristan chose the fresh strawberries and crème, this time along with a coffee. They waited for the waffles to be ready and then sat down at a table to eat.

"I could get used to these. Do they sell them in Minneapolis?" he asked.

"They're just starting to sell them in coffee shops and they will be at the State Fair next year."

"Maybe I can treat you to a waffle when we get back home?" He smiled sweetly and waited for her answer.

Her cheeks heated up. "You probably could persuade me to meet you for a waffle."

"I'll take that as a yes."

"Let's go find you a sweater," Annika said as she got up to toss her food wrappings in the trash bin.

Tristan dropped his trash in the bin and followed her to the next hall. She stopped at a rather large sweater shop which had quite a few selections.

She watched Tristan as he picked up a dark blue and white Dale sweater with a front quarter-zip opening. Annika liked what she saw. Tristan was definitely easy on the eyes, with his six foot, trim frame and dusty blond hair. And no one could miss those baby blue eyes, so it was no wonder he'd been drawn to the blue sweater.

"Slip it on and let's see how it fits," Annika said walking over to him.

"Okay." Tristan slipped it on over his shirt and walked over to check it in the mirror leaning against the wall. "What do you think?" he asked turning toward Annika.

"Matches your eyes. I think it's just your color. I like it. How about you?"

"Looks good. Does this make me look Norwegian?"

"Definitely. You'll fit right in now." Annika couldn't help smiling at him.

Tristan left the sweater on and handed the sales clerk his credit card after she removed the tags.

Annika browsed the ladies sweaters while she waited for him.

"Did you find anything that interested you?" Tristan asked walking up behind her.

"No, I'm good with the sweaters I have, which is actually five."

"Wow, it'll be tough keeping up with you."

"You know us women, we need one in each color. I only brought two on this trip. I purchased a black and red one, yesterday. I wore the brown and rust sweater yesterday. Today, I'm wearing the grey and white one my grandmother gave me."

"And you wear it very well. It's an eye-catching sweater. And if it's alright to say, I think you are an extremely attractive woman."

"Thank you." Annika felt her cheeks heating again and started walking toward the next booth. She took out her phone to check the time. "The Nordic Dancers will be performing in Valhalla Hall in fifteen minutes. If you'd care to join me, you're welcome to. They will be wearing their bunads, which are the traditional folk costumes typically made from wool with hand embroidered designs and adorned with unique silver pins called *Soljes*. Each region in Norway has a different color and design."

"I'd love to," Tristan said and followed her through the crowded hallways.

The performance stage sat at the far back end of the hall and was filling up fast. They found seats in the middle, about midway back from the stage.

Shortly after they were seated, the rest of the chairs were filled and people were also standing in the aisles on both sides and in the back. After a brief announcement about the Nordic Dancer's history, the dancers took the stage in their gorgeous hand embroidered bunads. Soon, the music could be heard and the dancers filled the whole stage performing dances from the old and past generations of Norway.

Annika was completely enthralled with the dancers. She enjoyed having Tristan along to share the experience with her. At least, she hoped he was enjoying it as much as she did. She glanced his way to find him engrossed in the show. It had been a long time since she'd done anything as a couple. But she needed to keep in mind they weren't a couple. In fact, they weren't even dating. *So what the heck am I doing? Being polite to a client, that's what.* Her biggest problem was enjoying it way too much. She didn't really know much about Matt, but she was glad those two ladies had taken up his morning.

Much too quickly, the show ended to a standing ovation of clapping people. They exited with the crowd and walked down the hallway to another food area to have lunch.

"So what new food are we going to try next?" Tristan asked taking in all the food offerings.

"I'm going to try one of the open-faced sandwiches." Annika walked up to a glass refrigerated case displaying the different options to choose from. "I'll take the smoked salmon," she said to the young girl behind the counter.

Tristan studied the sandwiches and chose the smoked salmon, also. They walked toward the tables and spotted Matt seated with a couple of young ladies from the tour. He waved for them to join him, so they made their way over to the table where he was seated and sat down.

"How's your morning going?" he asked.

"Great. Looks like you've made some new friends," Annika stated smiling at the ladies seated at the table.

"Yes, this is Sue and Tara," Matt introduced them.

Annika couldn't help noticing they too had chosen the open-faced sandwiches. "Nice to meet up with you. Hope you're enjoying the day at Hostfest."

"Oh, it's great having Matt join us. He's so interesting." Sue smiled toward Matt.

"I tried to catch up with you this morning, Annika," Matt said. "But I didn't have any luck. Fortunately, Sue and Tara invited me to join them. I'll be taking some pictures at the Nordic Sweater show. Will you be in the show?"

"I've done it before, but hadn't thought about it today. Tristan just bought a new sweater today, maybe he wants to be a part of it?" she asked looking directly at him.

"What do I have to do?"

"Just walk across the stage to model your sweater and give details about it."

"I just got it here today," he stated.

"Then, that is all you have to say. Some people will have hand-made sweaters. Some will have sweaters that have been passed down from other family members. Or some will have sweaters they personally bought on a trip to Norway."

"I will if you will. Then Matt can get pictures of both of us on stage," Tristan offered.

"Sure, why not? It'll be fun. We'll meet you at the Norsk Hall at four," Annika said.

Sue and Tara stood to leave grabbing Matt's hand and pulling him along with them.

"See you two later, then." Matt followed his ladies to the next hall.

"Well, looks like Matt has found some new friends," Annika stated.

"Yes, it does. That's the Matt I remember," he said.

"Care to clarify?"

"Matt was always the *Ladies Man*, if you catch my drift."

"Not exactly marriage material, I take it. Not that I'm looking to get married. At least not right now, anyway," Annika found herself stumbling over her words.

"Maybe in the future?" he asked smiling broadly.

"Well, of course," Annika said as she suddenly felt awkward. "I'd like to get married someday. Have a couple of kids. But right now, I need to focus on my new company."

"Oh, I hadn't realized you'd just started your company."

"Nordic Travel and Tours has been around for over thirty years. I've worked there for the past ten years and the owner just retired in January. He wanted it to go to the right person to take it forward, so he sold it to me. It's been a dream come true to run my own travel business and I have to give it 100% of my focus and time right now."

"From what I've seen of your expertise and passion for this business, I think you'll do quite well."

"Thank you. I take that as quite a compliment coming from a fellow business owner." Annika smiled.

"I'm sure when the right person comes along, you'll be able to divide your time between marriage and the business."

"I hope so. You never said but since I didn't see a ring, I assumed you weren't married. Are you married?"

Tristan laughed. "You certainly don't mince words. I like a woman who isn't afraid to speak her mind. No ring. No wife. Not married."

A wave of relief swept over Annika although she wasn't sure why. She wasn't interested in finding a husband and getting married at this point in her life, but she felt relieved in knowing he wasn't married. Instead, it meant he was most likely available. Of course, he could have a girlfriend. "Girlfriend?" She couldn't believe she'd just said it out loud.

"No girlfriend." Tristan chuckled.

Annika cleared her throat. "I think we have a Sweater show to sign up for." She got up and headed toward Norsk Hall. Although, she couldn't see Tristan, she sensed his movement behind her.

Once inside Norsk Hall, she made her way to the registration desk to sign up. "What do I need to fill out to be in the Sweater Show?"

"Just fill this out," the very Scandinavian older woman in her Norwegian sweater said. "I love your sweater," she stated. "Did you buy it in Norway?"

"No. Well, I didn't but my grandmother bought it for me on one of her trips to Norway."

"Are you going to join her in the show?" the lady at the desk looked over at Tristan.

Tristan nodded and took the slip of paper from her to fill out.

Matt walked up to the table. "So you both are going to be a part of the show?"

"Why not?" Tristan replied. "I have this new sweater, so might just as well be in the show with Annika."

The lady at the desk took the forms from them. "Please line up on the left side of the stage with the others."

Annika and Tristan made their way over to the line and Matt found a seat in the front row, so he could take pictures.

"Is this modeling?" Tristan asked.

"Sort of, but not really. You just talk about where or how you got your sweater, walk across the stage and do a couple of turns, so they can see the back of the sweater, too. After you're done, exit on the other side of the stage. Got it?"

"Sounds like there's nothing to it. You go first."

"Definitely. I'll show you how it's done."

"I can't believe I'm doing this," Tristan said as they watched the sweater show participants cross the stage one by one.

"My turn. See you on the other side," Annika said as she walked up the steps to the stage and the microphone. "My name is Annika Karlstad and I'm wearing a grey and white sweater hand-knit in Norway. It was given to me by my grandmother who purchased it on one of her trips to Norway." She slowly walked across the stage stopping twice to make a complete turn before descending the steps on the other side where she stopped to watch Tristan.

"My name is Tristan Torgersen and I am new to this whole sweater business. I purchased this sweater yesterday, here at Hostfest. It's a blue and white Dale sweater from Norway. I am glad to finally have one to wear to show my Norwegian heritage." He walked across the stage slowly, remembering to do two turns before exiting the stage.

"Good job," Annika said when he made his way to where she stood. She motioned to a couple of empty chairs where they sat down to watch the end of the sweater show.

Some people gave extremely interesting stories about how they'd obtained their sweaters. They both watched with interest until the last participant had crossed the stage. She'd noticed Matt had been busy snapping photos and recording the show to use for references in writing his article on Hostfest for the magazine. The two women, Sue and Tara were seated next to him, which hopefully meant they would keep him busy for the rest of the afternoon.

Tristan and Annika made their way back to the Viking Village to listen to a program on building the real Viking Village in Gudvangen, Norway. From the PowerPoint pictures, it definitely looked like someplace she'd like to visit in the near future. If it really looked as intriguing in person, she certainly would be adding it onto the Norway in a Nutshell tour her company offered.

"I think I'd like to visit Gudvangen, when or if I ever make it to Norway," Tristan remarked.

"You know I can make that trip happen. That's what I do." She grinned.

"I think I'm going to have to take you up on that," Tristan said.

Annika pulled out her phone to check the time. "We better head back to the Freya Hall. Dinner is at 5 pm in the En To Tre Restaurant."

This restaurant was a one of a kind fine dining restaurant where one could experience a taste of Scandinavia and it employed world class chefs from Norway. The evening meal featured a six-course culinary adventure including smoked salmon, duck, halibut and a delectable chocolate dessert. She couldn't wait to enjoy this special treat with Tristan.

"I have to admit, I'm feeling a bit lost, so lead the way," he said giving her a slight bow.

"Right this way." Annika looped her arm through his and led the way to Freya Hall.

Annika and Tristan were the first to arrive at En To Tre Restaurant. She walked up to the hostess stand to check in and pulled out her name list. The rest of their group arrived in small groups, were checked off her list, and seated by the hostess.

Last to arrive, was Matt with his entourage consisting of Sue and Tara. "Are we late?" Matt asked.

"No, but everyone else is already seated." Annika checked off their names and nodded to the hostess.

The hostess promptly seated them. She returned moments later and showed Annika and Tristan to a VIP table specially reserved for them.

"Wow. This is really top-notch treatment," Tristan said taking a seat across from Annika.

Shortly, a waiter appeared with the first of the six courses.

Annika noticed Tristan's gaze in the direction of Matt's table and caught Matt's scowl directed toward Tristan. She was about to say something when the next course appeared. As soon as they finished one course, the next one was brought to their table. Lastly, the fabulous chocolate dessert was placed in front of them.

After taking her first bite, Annika said, "This is what they call *To Die for Chocolate.*"

"I agree." Tristan said after sampling his dessert. "So what are the plans for after dinner?"

"There are none. We have about two hours left to do any last-minute shopping before the bus leaves for the hotel. Anything you still need to purchase?"

"I think I'm good, but I can always browse with you. Never know when you might see something you didn't know you needed."

Tristan's laugh was contagious and soon they were both laughing.

Almost everyone had already left, except for Matt's group who almost magically appeared at her and Tristan's table. "Fantastic meal! Got some great photos to use in the article, too."

"We're off to pick up a few more things before the bus leaves for the hotel. See you guys at the bus," Tara said as she pulled Matt with her and Sue.

Matt nodded his head as if to say he wasn't sure where they were going, but he would be following them.

"Do you think they have a threesome going?" Tristan asked.

Annika burst out laughing. "Definitely a possibility, if that's still a thing."

Tristan and Annika got up from the table and exited the restaurant. They meandered through the different halls, picking up a few more items each that they could use for Christmas presents.

Promptly at nine, after all the names were checked off her list, the tour bus left for the hotel. Everyone quickly exited the bus and walked to the lobby, then to their rooms.

Annika noticed Matt, Sue and Tara seated at the bar with drinks in front of them. She kept on walking to wait for the elevator where Tristan already stood.

The doors opened momentarily and they stepped in. Once it reached their floor, they exited.

"It was a memorable day. And night. I'm glad I was able to spend it with you," Tristan said when they stopped at the door to Annika's room.

Annika bestowed him with a lovely smile. "Me, too. Although, I'm exhausted, so I think I'm done for the day and my bed is calling me. That is, after I get my suitcase packed."

"Okay, I'll see you in the morning. Bright and early." Tristan stepped back to wait for her to open her door.

She did, entered her room and closed the door.

Why am I flirting with him? This would be a disaster in itself and it was out of line. Problem was she'd really had a great day and it was all because of Tristan. If, and that's a mighty big if, she was actually looking for a guy to date and fall in love with, he would be perfect. He was her client, she was focusing on her company and she'd made a promise. *No men for a year!* And she intended to keep her promise.

She swiftly packed her suitcase, put on her PJs and crawled into bed, falling asleep minutes later.

8

Tristan had trouble falling asleep. Visions of Annika's lips beckoned to him. He couldn't stop thinking about what it would be like to kiss her. His attraction to her was intense and overwhelming. She was the perfect woman for him, but he wasn't looking for a woman... or he hadn't been. So far, he'd been able to keep Matt away from her, thanks to Sue and Tara. Maybe both he and Annika would luck out and he would set his sights on one of them instead of her. Now, if he could just prevent himself from falling for her. He hadn't let anyone near his heart since Tonya.

The alarm went off in what seemed like only a few hours, as he hadn't fallen asleep for a long time after going to bed. He got up, showered, packed his suitcase, and headed down to the lobby. The bus was already loading the bags, so he took his to the loading area. Annika was busy at the bus's entrance door, checking off names. She looked his way so he nodded to her and walked back into the hotel lobby to grab some breakfast at the buffet. The bus would be leaving soon, so he opted for an egg and sausage breakfast sandwich and a coffee. He could see the bus through the window and people were still boarding, so he sat down to quickly eat before getting on the bus. He finished and made the bus just on time.

Everyone was finally on board, so the bus began its trek back to Minneapolis promptly at nine. It would take about twelve hours including stops for lunch and supper, with their arrival time home at about nine that evening. He took his seat across from Annika and once they were on the freeway, he promptly fell asleep leaning against the window with his neck pillow in place. His last vision of Annika was of her leaning against the window deep in thought, before his eyes closed. Time flew by as they passed mile after mile of the freeway leading to Minneapolis with a stop in Bismarck for lunch and Alexandria for dinner.

Finally, the bus pulled into the Eden Prairie transit station at nine-thirty where the passengers eagerly filed out to pick up their waiting bags.

Annika stayed by the bags until only a few remained. She looked around to see Matt walking towards her.

"Nice job on the tour," Matt said. "Very Minnesotan event. And North Dakotan, I guess. Say I never got to interview you, Annika. Can I catch up with you this week sometime?"

"I'll have to check my schedule. I think next week would be better, though."

"My story is due then and I'd like to include it in the article," Matt stated.

"Okay, well, call my office on Monday and I'll have Holly fit you in."

"Thanks." Matt nodded and walked towards the parking lot.

Only one suitcase besides hers remained on the curb. She looked up and saw Tristan waiting, although for what she wasn't sure.

He now moved toward their suitcases. "Well done. Excellent tour. Everything flowed nicely with no problems."

"Thank you." Annika pulled the handle up on her suitcase.

"I enjoyed our time together. I look forward to doing many more tours with you and your company." Tristan couldn't stop staring at her as he moved to stand in front of her.

Annika felt like he wanted to kiss her. It would be totally inappropriate, but she found herself wondering if he was a good kisser and if she would stop him.

He hesitated a moment as if reconsidering, then backed up a little. "I'll be in touch." He grinned at her, then turned and left.

Annika now stood on the curb alone, suitcase in hand. Obviously, he'd changed his mind. She was too tired to think about it right now, so she headed toward the parking lot to find her SUV, her suitcase rolling over the pavement behind her.

Monday morning, Annika arrived bright and early at her office. There was work to do and she wanted to get it done before Holly arrived.

Moments after her reports were finished, Holly walked into her office. "How was the Hostfest tour?" Holly asked taking a seat in Annika's office.

"Everything went quite smoothly."

"I know that. Expected that. You're a pro. What I want to know is how it went with the two guys?" Holly probed.

"Fine."

"That's all you have to say?"

"They're both nice guys from what I can tell. I spent the most time with Tristan since Matt was frequently preoccupied with two women from the tour."

"Okay, so what do you think of Tristan?"

"He's a very nice guy, but he's my client, so I can't go there."

"Darn."

Annika laughed. "What did you think was going to happen? Did you really think I'd change my mind about dating a client?"

"I was hoping."

"What's the status on the Lutsen tour?" Annika changed the subject.

"Everything is finalized with them."

"Great! Are the Fall Color tours full yet?"

"There's only one or two spots left on each one."

"Great, good job! Dana and Jack are set to lead those tours, correct?"

"Yes. The first one leaves this Friday morning, and everything is set."

"Matt will be calling, probably today sometime, to set up a meeting with me to do an interview. Try to put him off until next week if possible."

"He didn't get enough info from you on the tour?"

"I think there is some rivalry thing going on between Matt and Tristan. So ultimately, I ended up spending the majority of the time with Tristan."

"Tristan and Matt? They know each other?"

"Oh, sorry you didn't know. Yes, they went to college together, but haven't seen each other for a long time."

"That's quite interesting. Do you think they were friends back then?"

"Tristan said they were college roommates. But I have this feeling they didn't part ways on good terms for some reason, although I'm not sure."

"Well, I haven't met Matt, but I'm rooting for Tristan."

"Do you think they are competing to see who can win my attention?"

"Most certainly. But not attention, more like affection."

"Too bad, neither will be winning then. I'm not on the market, as the saying goes. At least not right now, anyway."

"Okay, if you say so. But your bet with your Paris friends is just that, it's a bet and it's okay to lose a bet. And you promised yourself a year to get Nordic Travel and Tours off the ground as *your* company and that will be on New Year's Eve."

"I think we're getting ahead of ourselves right now, neither one has even asked me out on an actual date, yet."

"Right, but mark my words, they will," Holly said as she walked out.

Later, that morning, Matt called to set up a time for his interview with Annika.

"Annika, I managed to push Matt off until Tuesday of the next week, his deadline was extended," Holly said, popping her head into Annika's office for a second, and then she returned to her office to answer the ringing phone.

Great, she had a week to prepare herself for meeting Matt again. He was definitely good looking, but she sensed he might be more of a ladies' man type instead of a good guy type. Regardless, she wanted to make a good impression on him. After all, he wrote for one of the top local magazines and his article could really get her company recognized in Minnesota. It would provide her with free publicity to her market area. Even if she wasn't really up for dating Matt, she'd be a fool to turn down his request for an interview of her personally and her company, Nordic Travel and Tours.

9

Tristan wanted nothing more than to call Annika. He wasn't sure why exactly, but after spending those days on the tour with her, it now felt like going cold turkey which amounted to no Annika. He enjoyed the time they'd spent together and wanted to spend more time with her. Just simply calling her and asking her to go out with him would be the easiest and most direct way of going about it, but there was always the chance, she'd say no. Then he'd have totally blown it. So he needed a different approach. He thought maybe her reluctance to encourage further contact had been because he was her client.

He'd almost blown their relationship by kissing her at the transit station. And man, had it taken a lot of self-control to walk away! Every fiber of his being wanted to take her in his arms to feel her body and lips pressed against his. He knew what he'd done was the right thing to do. Now, he needed to set up an appointment with her to discuss the tours he would be contracting with her company for the upcoming year for his members. From that meeting he hoped to secure a future date.

Tristan rose from his desk and walked over to the reception area.

"Britt, set up an appointment with Annika for this week sometime to go over our tour options for next year."

"Okay."

Tristan walked back to his office.

"Tristan, your appointment is Friday at two," Britt informed him over the phone.

"Thanks," he said and ended the call.

Tristan pulled into a parking spot at Nordic Travel and Tours a few minutes early for his two o'clock meeting on Friday. He walked into the reception area to find Annika and Holly deep in conversation and laughing.

Annika turned and saw him standing in the lobby. "So glad to see you, Mr. Torgersen. Let's talk in the meeting room."

He followed her down the hall. "It's been a crazy week, but I've been looking forward to this meeting with you."

"Take a seat, please. I've laid out our brochures for next year. Why don't you take a look at them and see which ones you think will be of interest to your members?"

He read them over to see which ones he thought would work for his company. "Iceland seems to be very popular with our younger members because it has quite an eclectic music scene. Prompted by this, they're interested in traveling all the way to a different country to attend one of Iceland's famous concerts." Tristan looked over at Annika.

Annika laughed. "Well, that is one reason to go to Iceland. But many people both young and old travel there to see the Viking artifacts, the geothermal springs or hot springs, the waterfalls, the countryside itself and the city of Reykjavik."

"Okay, I'll buy into all of that, too. I think Iceland would be a good choice." Tristan laughed.

"Any others places?" she asked.

"I think the Caribbean would be a good choice for the second trip. Maybe somewhere like Cancun?"

Annika grinned. "Cancun is my favorite winter destination. Airfare tends to be extremely reasonable, most hotels offer All-Inclusive packages so all the food and drinks are included. They tend to be very easy to work with as far as setting up group parties. Typically, we only offer the Scandinavian countries along with Europe, but I added the Caribbean when I took over the company."

"Send Britt, our travel coordinator, the dates and options for both of those destinations and she'll get back to you with our choices."

"I'll have Holly take care of it."

"Britt recommended to me that you should attend a couple of our in-town events so you can get the feel of what we offer our members and it would allow you to actually meet some of them and provide you the opportunity to talk to them, also."

"That's a very generous offer, but I don't think I would need to attend an event to book your travel." *That would be all she needed— spending more time with Tristan!*

"I think you're wrong. Attending one of our events is essential to our doing business together. I must insist." Tristan gave her his sexy smile.

Annika knew giving in to this particular demand, would be putting her heart in grave danger. She felt drawn to Tristan. He was one of the best-looking men she'd ever met in person. With the last name Torgersen, there was no denying he came from Scandinavian descent. He stood at over six feet tall and she knew from her own experience his chest was rock solid. Heck, he definitely came from Viking heritage. She could certainly envision him dressed as a Viking. Her thoughts halted. She wasn't looking for a man! When she'd made the promise to swear off men with her friends as a group bet, she had no idea she would then meet Mr. Right. Besides, she didn't have time for a boyfriend right now. "Sounds like I don't have a choice. So which event do you think I should attend?"

"How do you feel about costume parties?"

"Oh, I'm not sure..." Annika hesitated.

"We're hosting a Halloween costume party the Saturday before Halloween. In order to be sure everyone comes in costume, no one is allowed entrance unless they're wearing a costume. I'm sure you can come up with something. Can I plan on you attending?"

"I have no idea what to wear, but I guess I could find something that would qualify as a costume."

"Actually, we're hosting a party tonight. It's a casino night, so I better get back so I can help Britt set up." He stood, picked up the packet of brochures, and reached over to shake her hand.

As soon as his hand touched hers, she felt the heat from his hand flow through hers which was usually cold. He stood so close and his cologne smelled too good, she wanted to move even nearer and breathe in the distinct fragrance that was Tristan. It was a mistake. She should pull her hand back and move away from him, but she couldn't. For a moment, she thought he might kiss her.

Unfortunately or fortunately, depending on how she looked at the situation, he released her hand and headed out the door. "Talk to you later. Oh and if you feel like gambling tonight, stop by about seven." He continued walking down the hall and out the front door.

"More like taking a gamble on you." She was shocked she'd said it out loud. Thank heavens he was gone now. *Why even consider gambling tonight? Because then I could be around Tristan, that's why.*

Later in the afternoon, Tristan sent her an email with the address location for the Casino Night event, just in case she decided to stop by and check it out. It was at the RenWor Hotel on the west end of town which wasn't too far away from her office. She shook her head. He was definitely trying hard to spend time with her.

When she finally finished her reports and tour lists, it was already after six. She locked up the office and left. A few minutes later, she merged onto the freeway in the direction of the RenWor Hotel. Thankfully, she'd worn her red and black dress to work which would suffice for a casino party. *I've definitely lost my mind! Maybe I just need to convince myself that Tristan isn't the One for me.*

She found a parking spot and walked into the hotel where she immediately saw a large banner sign with Tristan's company name, *Minnesota Events and Adventures*. On the left side of the stairway was another large banner with Casino Night in large letters. At the top of the stairs, she approached a table where people were checking in.

"Your name?" the woman behind the table asked.

"I don't think my name is on your list. Tristan invited me."

"Oh, your name?" the woman asked again.

"Annika Karlstad."

"Annika, so happy to meet you! I'm Brittany Torgersen."

Annika hoped the shock on her face didn't show. Was Tristan really married? He'd said he wasn't. Maybe she'd totally mistook his words and actions and made more out of them than what really was going on. At this point, she was convinced she would die of embarrassment. Hell, he probably was only being polite when he'd invited her to the event. If only she could turn around and leave right now. Finally, she found her voice, "Pleased to meet you."

"Annika, you made it," Tristan said walking up behind her.

"Yes, but..." she paused looking toward Brittany.

"Oh, I see you met my sister." Tristan walked around the table, picked up the name tag with Annika's name on it, and handed it to her.

Brittany nodded. "I'm so glad we'll be working together with your company. I'm the office manager so I do all the travel and tour coordinating. Doing business with Nordic Travel will make my job considerably easier. Tristan, show her our Casino Night games. Have fun, you two."

"Thank you," Annika replied.

Tristan held out his arm for her to take as he escorted her into the ballroom.

He looked like a model for a magazine in his perfectly tailored black tuxedo. Her hormones were going crazy and touching him was driving her crazy. But she couldn't pull away from him without appearing rude.

"This is what our standard Casino Night looks like. We have Black Jack, Poker, Texas Hold-Em, and a Roulette wheel. What would you like to try?" Tristan picked up a bag of chips for each of them and waited for her answer.

"I'm kind of partial to Black Jack, if that's okay?"

They took a seat at the Black Jack table.

Annika looked around the room and saw men and women of all ages laughing and having a good time. It appeared to be a safe and good way to meet people. She wondered how many actually ended up as couples.

"Black Jack," the dealer said to her as he set chips in front of her and took her cards.

Tristan was the perfect gentleman the entire evening as they went from game to game. She had accumulated quite a stack of chips and was able to exchange them for a gift certificate to see a play at the Ordway Theater.

"I should get going," Annika said.

They walked to the hotel lobby together. "Let me walk you to the parking lot," he offered.

She hesitated.

"It's dark and I want you to be safe. Of course, if you'd rather I didn't..." Tristan hesitated, waiting for her answer.

"No. I mean yes, that would be great."

They walked out the door to the parking lot.

"Thanks. I had a great time." Annika stopped and pressed the button to open the door to her SUV.

"I'm glad you came," Tristan said and backed away as she got in, then he turned and went back to the hotel.

Annika watched him walk away thinking any woman would be lucky to end up with him. Though the real question going through her mind was, could that woman be her?

10

The following Tuesday morning, Matt arrived promptly at Nordic Travel and Tours for his interview with Annika.

"So Matt, I'm not sure what exactly you would like to discuss during this interview?"

"I want to know about you, how you got into the travel business, and how you came to own Nordic Travel and Tours," Matt said and took a seat at the table in the meeting room.

"Okay, but what is the theme of this article for Minnesota Events Magazine?" Annika asked taking her seat at the head of the meeting table.

"Oh, sorry, I wasn't clear about that. We're featuring women business owners in the Metropolitan area. Essentially, we tell a story about you and your business, which will hopefully bring your company business. It's free marketing and advertising."

"Do I get final approval on the article before it goes to print?" she asked.

"Of course, I'll send you a copy before it is submitted for the January edition."

"Well, let's get started. Ask away," Annika said and leaned back in her chair for the inquisition to begin.

"Have you always wanted to be in the travel business?"

"I've always loved traveling to see new places. My dad was a pilot and my mom was a flight attendant, they're retired now and live in Phoenix. Having flight perks was something my parents took full advantage of. My brother and I traveled all over the world with them. So basically, travel was in my blood."

"Did you go to college?" he asked.

"Yes, I graduated from St. Olaf College in Northfield with a degree in Mass Communications and a minor in History."

"What was your first job in the travel industry?"

"I started working for American Express travel during college. I worked for them for a couple of years and then moved to Nordic Travel and Tours after graduation. It was a small travel company focused on the Scandinavian countries. My great-grandparents came from Norway, so it seemed like a perfect fit. I'd been to the Scandinavian countries many times through the years with my family to visit distant relatives. The fjords of Norway are unbelievable, if you ever have the chance to see them, do it. Mostly, I wanted the opportunity to help other people see these exquisite countries. Dan Nystad who owned Nordic Travel and Tours, trained and mentored me for the past ten years. He recently retired in January of this year and sold me the company."

After many more questions, the interview ended two hours later.

"I'll be working on this starting tomorrow and should be able to get you a copy to review by Thursday. Does that sound all right with you?"

"That'll be fine, I'll look it over as soon as I receive it and get it back to you within 24 hours." Annika walked Matt to the door and he left.

He'd acted totally professional the whole time and had even made her feel at ease with his questions. None had seemed too personal, which was what she'd been leery of. Matt was definitely easy on the eyes, but he hadn't led her to believe he wanted anything more than a business type relationship. *Since he wasn't exactly a client, it would be okay to go on a date with him, right? No! Not right.* She wasn't dating anyone for a year, she'd promised her friends.

Promptly on Thursday morning, she received an email from Matt with an attachment containing the article he'd written for the magazine. She opened it and read the document. He'd done a wonderful job and she approved of every word in it. This article could possibly bring in local business which would definitely benefit Nordic Travel and Tours. Quickly, she sent him a reply signing off on the article.

His reply came back within seconds thanking her for her authorization to print the article. To her surprise, it included an invitation to accompany him to a VIP pre-opening of the Ice Castle in Excelsior being featured in a new article he was working on for the magazine. It was on the first Friday in November.

Her mind was in turmoil. Why didn't this happen, when she was looking for someone to date? Now, she possibly had two men interested in her, when she'd sworn off dating. Well, one date wouldn't qualify as dating or having a boyfriend and besides, the Ice Castle sounded interesting. She sent her reply stating she'd be happy to join him.

The following week she went shopping for a Halloween costume. She really hated costumes and wasn't sure why she'd agreed to attend the event. Actually, she was having second thoughts about going. However, she did want to see Tristan. She enjoyed spending time with him, but it was similar to walking on shaky ground as far as her promise went. Finally, on Thursday, she found a Medieval Renaissance style dress that would work. She would also be able to wear it to the Renaissance Festival held every year in August, also.

Saturday was her lazy day at home time. She cleaned, did laundry, then relaxed with a glass of wine. Around six, she went to her bedroom to change into her costume. The Halloween Party would be taking place at the same hotel as the Casino Night event, which was close to her condo. She arrived fashionably late at seven-thirty.

Brittany was seated at the check-in table with Tristan hovering over her shoulder dressed in a Viking costume. He looked like a real Viking, at least she thought that's what they looked like according to the TV Viking show she watched. Man, he was so dang handsome.

He looked up just as she approached the table. "Annika! I love your costume," he reached around Brittany and checked off her name.

"Thanks." Annika smiled at him.

He came around the table and took her hand to lead her into the ballroom.

It was a bold move and she wasn't sure what she should do. He seemed so happy to see her. Desire danced in his eyes, so she let him guide her into the hauntingly and eerily decorated room.

Someone had spent a lot of time decorating. It was obvious. A stage stood at the back of the room with a band, playing cover songs everyone knew and could easily dance to. Food tables lined the walls filled with spooky and ghoulish styled delectables. A cauldron styled bowl was filled with some concoction which probably contained alcohol. Various game stations were set up where the members could play games to win prizes.

"Are you hungry?" he asked pointing to the food tables.

"Yes, I didn't have supper," she answered.

They filled their plates and took a seat at a table.

He left for a few minutes to get them drinks and returned shortly. "So how was your week?" he asked.

"Busy. How about yours?"

"I've been extremely busy getting ready for this party and putting up decorations. So what do you think?"

"Looks great. There seems to be a lot of people here. I didn't realize you had this many members."

"Yes, it's one of our bigger events, so we usually get a big turnout," he said.

They ate and played games. Tristan won her a stuffed animal which wasn't actually an animal but a pumpkin. The band played

Michael Jackson's song, *Thriller,* and the dance floor filled quickly. Annika began moving to the beat of the song and singing along.

"I think you need to dance to this one," Tristan said taking her hand and leading her to the dance floor.

"Yes, I love it," she said and began dancing as soon as they reached the dance floor area.

They danced to the next few songs and when the song changed to a slow song, he silently asked approval waiting with open arms. She moved into them and he drew her to his chest. Their bodies fit nicely, meshing together perfectly. He smelled so masculine and she knew he could become a huge distraction, which could cause her to lose the bet and not keep the promise she'd made. Annika wondered how her friends were doing with the *no men thing. Were they having as many second thoughts about it as me?* Right now, she wanted nothing more than for him to kiss her.

Annika looked up into Tristan's eyes. Could it be love she saw? No, it couldn't be. Heck, they barely knew each other. But it definitely was something. While she was having this conversation with herself, Tristan tipped her chin up with his fingers and gently pressed his lips against hers. She welcomed the kiss and returned it as passion ignited throughout her body.

It ended all too soon as he released her and stared into her eyes waiting for a response.

She said nothing. She couldn't, it was almost as if she was in shock. Thank heavens, it was dark in the ballroom, but she couldn't help wondering if anyone had seen him kiss her. Thankfully, they were in costume. Maybe no one knew who they really were anyway.

He took her hand, led her into the hallway and down an empty corridor. Stopping at the end, where it was somewhat secluded, he stared deeply into her eyes. "Annika, I'm sorry. I was out of line. And completely unprofessional. All I can say in my defense is you are a very beautiful and intriguing woman and I simply got lost in the moment." Tristan stood merely a few feet from her.

"It was my fault, too. I could've walked away, but I didn't. I do think, however, going forward we should keep this professional since we will be working together." She felt nervous and clasped her hands together.

"I agree. It's just too bad I really enjoy spending time with you." This time he smiled wickedly at her.

"Me, too. Which is exactly why I'm going to call it a night." Annika turned and walked away before she changed her mind.

Tristan could do nothing but watch her leave.

11

The following week, she received an email from Tristan, asking if she'd ever attended a Lutefisk dinner. This crazy thing called *Lutefisk* was the talk of the town this time of year. He'd heard there were many of these dinners being held in the local Lutheran Churches around the Twin Cities. Some of his members had even mentioned them and suggested he set up a Lutefisk Dinner as an event for the month of December and could she help him.

This would be a perfect opportunity to justify calling him. She pressed his number into the phone on her desk. "Hello, this is Annika."

"So happy to hear your voice. Did you get my email?"

"Yes. And yes, I've been to many Lutefisk Dinners. One of my favorite ones is next week on Saturday at St. John's Lutheran Church in Lakeville."

"Really. One of my members suggested we put one on the calendar for December, but I'm a little hesitant to do it since I've never attended one. In fact, I'm not totally sure what they are exactly or if they even take reservations for groups. And since you are the only Scandinavian expert I know, I thought maybe you could give me some insight into them."

Annika laughed. "I think I need to get an extra ticket for you to join me next Saturday."

"If you're inviting me, I accept. But I have to say I've heard some pretty bad stuff about the *Lutefisk*."

"You'll have to try it for yourself! I'll email you the address and you can meet me there. It's at six."

"Thanks so much for inviting me, even though I kind of invited myself. But I really didn't know where to start looking to find one. It seems like it's a Lutefisk secret society and you have to know someone to find out about them."

"You can be pretty funny sometimes, Tristan. I think the issue is most of them are held at Lutheran Churches in their basements and they don't post them on the internet, so they'd be hard to find, unless like you said, you know someone."

"Exactly."

"They're kind of a Norwegian sweater event, too. Most people, who have sweaters, wear them. I'll be wearing mine, so you can wear your new sweater from HostFest, if you want."

"I think I will. I don't want to be the only one *not* wearing a sweater. Okay, I'll see you next week on Saturday night. Sorry to cut this short, but Britt just reminded me I have a meeting in five minutes."

"No problem. See you Saturday." Annika ended the call. *Did I just ask him on a date?* She was supposed to be trying *not* to see him, but this was strictly business. She was helping out one of her clients. At least that's what she told herself as far as excuses went.

Before she knew it, Friday night arrived and she was on her way to the VIP Pre-Opening of the Ice Castle in Excelsior to meet Matt. Her *not dating anyone* situation had been elevated to *not dating two* very hot eligible men. However, she was looking forward to seeing the Ice Castle.

Matt was waiting for her at the entrance to the VIP tent. He looked cold, as the temps were in the mid-twenties. When he saw her walking towards the tent, he approached her and gave her a quick hug as a greeting. "This way," he said leading her through the crowd.

"The Ice Castle is unbelievable, I've never seen anything like this," she said.

"Wait until we see the inside, I've heard it's almost like being in the ice castle from the kid's movie, *Frozen*."

"Well, then I can't wait to see it."

Matt stopped at the check in table to get name badges for them and then they moved inside the tent, complete with an ice bar where drinks were being offered. Blue Ice Curacao was served in clear glasses with a semi cube surface to make them look like ice cubes. They saw a fake ice fishing game where you could pretend to catch fish, via ice fishing. Everyone was handed a bag upon entering which contained a long sleeved T-shirt portraying a picture of an ice castle on the front side. She eyed a table filled with cold shrimp appetizers on ice and over to the other side of the tent a sushi bar. Desserts were mini shaped ice cream ice castles served in a dish. Everything else was finger foods, so they could be easily carried around.

They sampled everything and then followed the crowd to the actual Ice Castle.

"Did you know the Ice Castle is actually made with 10,000 plus icicles?" Matt asked.

"No, I didn't. This is amazing," Annika answered and continued looking at all the icicles in awe.

"Also, they use thousands of LED lights throughout the castle to cast lighting in various colors."

"It sounds like you've done your homework," she said.

"Research is key to a top-notch article," Matt stated proudly.

The castle was over thirty feet high and boasted ice carved slides and tunnels. Matt walked beside her the whole time and she felt leery of holding his hand, but after almost slipping a couple of times, she decided it would be the safer option. He'd been the perfect gentleman, but it was obvious he considered it a date.

As they were leaving the event, he offered to accompany her to the west end parking lot, but she declined due to the cold temps. The winds had picked and sent the temperature plummeting to a negative ten wind-chill. She remotely started her SUV from the tent so it was starting to warm up when she got in. After cranking up the heat, she turned on her seat warmers. Why did she feel bad for running out on Matt? She'd left abruptly, because she had a feeling he was about to kiss her. Although, a part of her wanted to see if she liked his kiss as much as she'd liked her kiss with Tristan.

Annika's week was busy but she managed to slip some time in to get a list of Lutefisk Dinners coming up in December. She made a few calls to see which were the larger ones and were able to take reservations for a group. She found out Good Shepherd Lutheran Church in Minneapolis would be able to make a reservation for 25 to 50 people for their dinner on the Sunday after Thanksgiving. It was coming up quickly though, so she wasn't sure it would be a viable option for Tristan's group. She sent him off a quick email with all the info. It was Thursday already, so she would talk to him about it on Saturday.

Saturday arrived before she knew it and she was meeting Tristan for dinner. But no way would she count a Lutefisk Dinner as a date. It was strictly business. Honestly though, she couldn't deny that she'd been looking forward to seeing him. She picked her red and black Oda sweater from Norway which was made from the thinner new lightweight wool to go with a pair of black jeans and a pair of black boots. The weather was still chilly, somewhere in the teens, so she grabbed a lightweight black down insulated puffy coat on her way out to her SUV.

There would be various seating times for the dinner. She had tickets for six o'clock. When she walked into the church foyer, she saw Tristan already waiting for her.

He wore his sweater and had a huge smile for her. It made him look very Scandinavian and extremely handsome.

"I like your sweater," Tristan said as he moved towards her.

"Thank you and you look very Scandinavian in yours," she replied.

"I'm thinking the strong odor I smell in here is the Lutefisk, right?" he asked.

Annika burst out laughing. "Yes, it is. After you are in here awhile, you won't even notice it anymore."

"The light at the end of the tunnel."

They were both laughing as they walked into the church to take a seat on a pew.

"We're now seating for six, so please give me your tickets as you enter through this door," a man announced from the front of the church.

"That's us." Annika nodded.

They got in line and handed their tickets to the man then followed the group into the church basement. A woman dressed in a traditional day bunad, motioned for them to sit at table ten. A family of six, mother, father, grandmother, grandfather and two teenaged children joined them. They claimed Norwegian and Swedish heritage and they all loved lutefisk. The servers brought out the meal consisting of lutefisk, meatballs, boiled potatoes, coleslaw, lefse, rommegrot (similar to a warm white pudding) all served family style. They were offered water, lemonade, or coffee to drink. Lastly, dessert platters were brought out filled with Scandinavian Christmas Cookies—krumkake, sandbakels, kringlas, goros, and almond cake.

Tristan held the plate of lutefisk in his hand, staring at the gelatin like fish. "This is it?"

"Yes, now you have to at least try one bite."

Reluctantly, he lifted a small portion onto his plate. The meatballs on the other hand smelled delicious, so he took a large spoonful. "Which sauce do I use?" he asked looking from the butter sauce to the cream sauce.

"I opt for both. It kind of kills the taste a little and makes it easier to get down."

Tristan now had lutefisk smothered in butter and white sauce. Hesitantly, he lifted the fork to his mouth, chewed and swallowed.

"How is it?" She smirked.

"I can honestly say I've never tasted anything like it before." He frowned, then smiled and began laughing.

"Hey, but the rest looks appealing, so it's uphill going forward!"

"Let's hope so." He laughed.

They proceeded to try the other foods, which were delicious.

"I think my members would enjoy this as a Minnesota Scandinavian experience. I hope we aren't too late and have missed them all by now."

"You may be in luck." Annika replied. "I found one on the Sunday after Thanksgiving. Everyone should've had their fill of turkey by then and will be looking for something else to eat. It's at Good Shepherd Lutheran Church in Minneapolis and they would be able to take a reservation for 25 to 50 people for their dinner. It's kind of short notice."

"Oh, my members are spontaneous. I'll let Britt know right away and she'll get it out to the membership by tomorrow. We'll see what response we get."

As they walked out of the church basement and up the steps to the exit, they passed many people wearing their Scandinavian sweaters, showcasing a diverse display of color hues and designs, making each one unique. At the door, they paused to put on their coats. It had been one of those odd years when the temps had dropped quickly, although it hadn't snowed yet, but everyone knew it would be coming.

"So, how is your next week looking?" Tristan opened the door and they walked to the parking lot under the glowing lights sporting ice crystal halos.

"Probably busy and hectic. Oh and Holly's baby is due next Saturday. So then I will be even busier."

Stopping in front of her running SUV, they stood too close for her *no boyfriend policy*.

"Thanks for inviting me. It was an interesting experience, but yet it was a new adventure of sorts," he explained. "And that's my thing, trying new things whenever possible."

"Glad you enjoyed it." She looked up into his blue eyes dancing with excitement. "I can tell you like adventures. And maybe new challenges?"

"Always." He grinned at her. "Better get in before the engine turns off, you look a bit cold."

"Yes, I am." She turned around so she could open the door.

"Send me the info on the Lutefisk Dinner as soon as possible, so I can have Britt get the advertisement out to the group."

She nodded, got in the SUV and as she shut the door, he was already walking away. Being kissed in a parking lot when it was barely thirty degrees out wasn't the ideal situation, so why did she feel like she'd missed out on something really great? She remembered the kiss at the Halloween party and knew she definitely wanted more kisses from this man. Yes, she knew exactly what she'd just missed out on.

12

On Wednesday morning, shortly after Annika arrived at the office, Holly's husband, Tom, called to say they were on their way to the hospital because her water had just broke. The week had already been hectic and flown by but going forward it would be even busier since they were coming up on the Christmas season. She immediately sorted through the files Holly left on her desk in anticipation of not being there. Unfortunately, Becca, who had initially been training to fill in for Holly, had left a couple of weeks earlier to take a permanent position at another travel company. Thankfully, they'd hired a new temp, Jessica, who would be filling in while Holly was out on maternity leave and she'd just arrived.

"Jessica, looks like you're on your own now. Holly is at the hospital and hopefully, will be delivering her baby soon."

"Don't worry, she filled me in on everything at the beginning of the week." Jessica hung up her coat and sat down at her desk.

"Great. We will be going ahead with the Lutefisk dinner for the Events and Adventures group on the Sunday after Thanksgiving. Make sure they have everything they need."

"Yes, I have all the info for that event right here," Jessica said and picked up a folder from her desk.

"I sent the info to Britt on Monday so she could get everything put on their website and start taking reservations." Annika breathed a sigh of relief as she walked back to her office. "Let me know if you have any questions."

Annika started going through her emails and spotted one from her mother. Her parents wanted her to come to Phoenix for Thanksgiving. She hadn't spent much time with them this year since she'd been so busy with her new company. It was something she needed to do, make time for her family. She missed them immensely. Flights wouldn't be cheap at this late date, but she managed to find a reasonable one. The flight left on Wednesday afternoon and returned the Saturday after Thanksgiving. Once she'd forwarded the itinerary to her mom, she proceeded to work her way down the long list of emails.

She spotted one from Matt—an invitation for Saturday night. He wanted to know if she was interested in attending the Holidazzle Parade being brought back due to the overwhelming public outcry after it ended a few years ago. It was something she'd intended to see for years but something else had always been more important and taken priority. Spending time with Matt had been pleasant enough, so the idea that he had thought to invite her made Annika feel good. Maybe, he wasn't such a bad guy after all.

Regardless whether or not she had any feelings for him, she wasn't about to miss another chance to see the Holidazzle Parade. The downtown area would already be decorated for Christmas and that alone would be worth seeing. She hadn't managed to go downtown during the Christmas season for the last couple of years, either. What with Dayton's department store closing, which had also meant no more Santa Bears, and the parade ending, she hadn't felt motivated. She certainly didn't want to pass on this opportunity though. Her reply went out to Matt, accepting his invitation.

Further down the list was a reminder invitation for an upcoming weekend event, only it was on Sunday afternoon, to attend the Swedish Institute's Nordic Christmas Opening Night Tour which she'd attended the past few years. *Alone.* She'd always gone solo. It would be so nice to finally bring someone, not necessarily a date, but maybe a business associate? *Did she dare invite Tristan?* Wondering why she hadn't noticed the original invitation, she checked her spam folder and found it. She didn't have much time, but she'd have to think about it. Get her courage up to ask him.

Just before five, she received a call from Tom, informing her that Holly had given birth to a healthy baby girl, weighing seven pounds five ounces. They would be naming her Elsa. Both Holly and the baby were doing fine. Annika was happy for her friend and co-worker, who'd wanted a baby for over three years. Finally, it was a reality and she would stop by the hospital on Friday to visit both of them.

After lunch on Friday, Annika stopped by Target to pick up a baby gift, along with something for Holly. The hospital was only a few minutes from the office, so she decided to take the rest of the after-noon off and make her stop now.

The elevator doors opened and she pressed seven for the Mater-nity floor. Her hands were full carrying flowers and two gift bags. She knocked on the door to Holly's room before entering. "It's me, Annika."

"Come in," Holly replied.

Annika walked in setting her packages on the window sill area. "How are you doing?" she asked turning toward Holly.

"I'm not going to say delivering a baby is easy, but it went fairly smooth. No complications. Really glad it's over, though!"

"I bet. Can't imagine what it's like, since I've never had a baby. You look good. How's Elsa doing?"

"Good. Everyone said to let her stay in the nursery, so I can get some sleep. I guess you don't get any sleep when you get home."

"That I've heard from many friends who've had babies. Sounds like a good idea to let the nurses take care of her and get as much sleep as you can."

"How's Jessica doing?"

"So far, no problems. I miss you, though." Annika smiled at Holly.

"Any new developments with the *no men policy*?"

"You would ask that. Well, let's see. The Ice Castle was incredible and Matt was a total gentleman. The Lutefisk dinner was fun with Tristan."

"Neither tried to get a kiss?"

"No, sorry. Kind of wished Matt had so I could see if we have any chemistry."

"Meaning you *do* have chemistry with Tristan?" Holly smiled.

"Maybe. Sort of. He's my client though. Makes it difficult."

"I know. But sometimes you just have to take a chance."

The door opened and the nurse pushed in the cart with Holly's baby. "It's almost time to try nursing her." The nurse picked up Elsa, completely wrapped like a mummy in a pink blanket, and gave her to Holly. "Call me if you need anything." She quietly left the room.

Annika walked over to the bed to take a peek at the tiny face hidden inside the blanket. "She's adorable, Holly."

"Thanks, I think so, too. Just think if you take a chance on Tristan, you could be holding your own baby in a couple of years."

"So it's Tristan, not Matt, who's your favorite?" Annika asked.

"They're both good looking, professional and likeable men. But I like Tristan for you."

"Why is it when I'm looking I can't even get a date and when I'm not, I have two guys asking me out?"

"I think that's the way it works. Wait a minute. Did they ask you out again?"

"Matt did. Seems this weekend is popular. He invited me to a VIP Holidazzle Parade event downtown that's tomorrow, Saturday."

"And?"

"I accepted. Mainly because I want to see the parade."

"See, I think you like Tristan better, too."

"I'm thinking about asking Tristan to attend the Swedish Institute's Christmas event with me on Sunday. I missed the original invite and just received the reminder on Wednesday. I've gone the past years alone, but I thought it might be nice to bring someone this year."

"Yes! Invite him. I'm betting he'll say yes."

The baby started to get restless and began crying.

"I'd better let you feed her. I'm going to pick up something to eat on my way home and chill out in front of the TV. I hear there are some new Hallmark Christmas movies out already."

"Okay. Thanks for stopping by. Oh, and let me know how the weekend goes with your two guys."

"I'll let you know." Annika smiled as she walked out of the room to the sounds of Elsa crying.

She couldn't help stopping in front of the large window to the Baby Nursery, where three babies were lined up so you could see them up close. They were so tiny and precious. Miraculous gifts from God. She'd always been drawn to babies and was usually the first one to ask permission to hold them. More than anything, she'd always dreamed of having a family. Unfortunately, she'd let her career come first. Now she had her own company and it was off to a great start, maybe she could start thinking about beginning a relationship and then possibly starting a family. Of course, first she needed to find a husband. To find one of them, she needed to, let one of them or both, spend time with her. Like Tristan and Matt. Instinct told her she wasn't going to win the *no men* bet with her friends.

13

After eating her pasta takeout meal, she emailed Tristan the info on the Swedish Institute's event on Sunday. Immediately, she set her phone on the kitchen counter and went to change into comfy pajamas to watch a Christmas movie. She turned the TV on, found her happy channel and settled in on the couch, deliberately leaving the phone in the kitchen so she wouldn't be tempted to keep checking for his reply.

Midway through the movie, she got up to pour herself a glass of wine and noticed it was lightly snowing outside. They would only get flurries if the weatherman was right. She glanced toward the phone and couldn't resist picking it up. Never had she invited a client to an event on a personal level. She was *so* out of her comfort zone. Slowly, she turned it over and saw she had a new email. She tapped the phone to read the message and Tristan's reply popped on the screen. He accepted her invitation and asked her to send him the details. Quickly, she sent him the time and address. Relief spread through her body as she sat down on the couch and pressed play on the movie. She had a date with Tristan. A smile spread across her face as she took a sip of wine and snuggled under her blanket to watch the end of the movie. These movies always had happy endings and maybe it was time she got one, too.

Since it snowed overnight and the temps were in the twenties, Annika chose her flannel lined jeans, warmest boots and a long down filled coat for Saturday evening's event. They would be sitting outside for the two hours it would take for the parade to pass by the VIP section which offered heated seat pads and heated blankets. She felt glad they were provided so she didn't have to spend the day searching the stores to buy them. It was her lucky day. She promptly found a curbside parking spot only one block from the Nicollet Mall. The Holidazzle Parade started on the Nicolet Mall at Sixth Street where the VIP bleachers were located. On the same corner was a Caribou Coffee shop where she was meeting Matt to first pick up a couple of hot chocolates.

He stood waiting outside the door when she arrived and looked very attractive in his Paul Bunyan style coat, hat and gloves. A huge sexy grin greeted her.

Matt leaned toward her to give her a hug. "It's good to see you. I'm glad you came dressed for the weather, I think it's going to be a bit cold tonight."

"I'm a Minnesota girl. I definitely know how to dress for this weather. Staying warm is my primary goal." She laughed.

He opened the door and they immediately got in line to order their drinks. The shop was crowded, but the line was moving quicker than expected and before she'd warmed up, they'd picked up their drinks.

"It'll be starting soon, so we should find our seats." He reached out to take her free hand to lead her through the crowd to the bleachers.

They had good seats and promptly sat down, turning on the heat, both on their seats and blankets.

"I may be starting to get a little warmer," Annika commented. "I can't image standing out here for two hours without these heated seats and blankets. I think I'd be frozen in less than thirty minutes."

"It sounds like you haven't watched the parade before?" Matt asked.

"Nope. Never made it down here before, so thanks for inviting me. It's something I've always wanted to do."

"My pleasure. Glad you could make it. Oh look, here comes the first float."

A Gingerbread House drove by. The parade consisted of twelve floats total, boasting of more than 350,000 lights. Even a Metro Transit bus, literally covered in lights was part of the parade.

"I think I like the Christmas Train best, with Santa's sleigh a close second," Annika stated with her eyes fixated on all the colorful lights.

"They are certainly the kids' favorites," Matt commented and looked her way.

"Maybe, I'm just a kid at heart." She laughed. "Who doesn't like Santa?"

"I think that's the end of the parade. Would you like to go inside somewhere to get warm and get a bite to eat?"

"Sure. Where do you want to go?" she asked.

"Britt's Pub is just a half of block away. They have good food."

"Let's go. The heat is calling me."

Matt took her gloved hand to help her down the bleacher steps, but didn't release it as they began walking briskly toward their destination.

She wasn't sure how she felt about it, but with the thick gloves, they were wearing it seemed quite harmless.

They managed to get a table in the back corner and ordered two Shepherd Pies which Britt's Pub was famous for, along with Guinness Beers.

Annika hung her coat on the back of her chair as she was finally warming up and Matt did the same.

"So what did you think of your first Holidazzle Parade?" he asked.

"I loved it! Even if it was a bit cold outside."

"Did you know it started way back in 1992?" Matt inquired.

"Wow! Can't believe I never made it down here before."

"It was inspired by the extravagant Walt Disney parades. Downtown merchants were concerned the opening of the Mall of America would take away their customers, so Dayton's and Brookfield Development along with the City of Minneapolis put in the startup money. The Dayton's 8th floor auditorium Holiday Show always opened the first night of the parade."

"I didn't know that. My mom always took me to Dayton's to see the show and Santa, of course. I loved going. I guess we always went during the day, so we were never down there when the parade was taking place."

"Just a little trivia for you. Did you know Dayton's started their holiday shows in 1963 and ended in 2016? They definitely had a good run and made a lot of children happy through the years."

"I didn't know it was a tradition for that many years. How do you know all of this downtown Minneapolis trivia?"

"I'm a writer. I did an article on Dayton's a few years back and now, I'm doing one on the Holidazzle Parade, which is how I got the VIP tickets. I'm a hard-core researcher when I write articles on events. Here comes our food."

The food was quickly consumed. One would've thought they were starving. Matt offered more research facts relating to other magazine articles he'd written. The Pub had a long waiting line for tables so they chose not to loiter.

"Where are you parked? I'll walk you to your car," Matt offered once they were back bundled up and outside.

"This way." She pointed and they strode onward at a fast pace as the temps had dropped even more.

The streets were still crowded with people from the parade, but shortly they were in front of her SUV. She pressed the auto start button.

"Thanks for joining me. You're great company, Annika."

"I had a great time. I'm checking the Holidazzle Parade off my bucket list. I'm not even going to guess what the wind chill is, but it's dang cold out here. Where are you parked? I can give you a ride to your car." She didn't wait for his response, instead immediately opened the door. "Get in," she said as she closed her door and unlocked the passenger door.

Matt got in. "It is really cold out there. Thanks. My car is just a couple of blocks away. Take a right at the corner, go three blocks and it will be on the right. A black Cadillac Escalade."

Annika took off her gloves and tossed them along with her purse in the back seat. Within minutes, they arrived where Matt's Escalade was parked.

There were cars behind her waiting, so he jumped out quickly. "Thanks, I'll be in touch," he said as he closed her door, opened his and slid inside.

She slowly merged into the traffic and headed for the freeway entrance.

Once home, she shed her winter outerwear, slipped into her warm pajamas and crawled into bed. She was exhausted. The evening had been a success and she really couldn't fault Matt on anything. He'd been a perfect gentleman. No kiss, but then there really hadn't been an opportunity. She was really looking forward to seeing Tristan tomorrow, and his smiling face was the last thing on her mind before she fell asleep.

14

The winds let up so there wasn't as much of a wind chill on Sunday when she left to meet Tristan. She wore a modern, lighter weight Vrikke Norwegian sweater that tended to be a sleeker fitting classy style. The red and black colors lent toward a Christmas look with black legging jeans and black leather heeled boots. *I'm dressing to impress which says what? That I like Tristan?* She did, even if she didn't want to admit it.

When she approached the check in table, she saw him waiting, wearing his recently acquired Norwegian sweater. He seemed to be getting a lot of use out of his purchase but she was thinking he needed to obtain a second one. Regardless, he looked smoking hot. He was one good looking Nordic guy with the high sculpted cheek bones and he definitely wore the five o'clock shadow well. She didn't miss Tristan admiring her at the same time.

He walked toward her. "Annika. You look good. I like your sweater." He smiled.

"I like yours, too." She stepped up to the table to get their name tags and the itinerary.

"So what's first?" he asked while pinning on his name tag.

"First, we tour the Christmas rooms, each decorated in the traditions of one of the Nordic countries-Sweden, Denmark, Finland, Iceland and Norway."

"So we follow the arrows, then?" He held out the crook of his arm for her.

Annika looped her arm in his as they began their Christmas journey through the Nordic countries. They moved leisurely through each room stopping to read the signs explaining the meanings behind the traditions. Lastly, they walked into the Norway room. The Christmas tree was decorated with little Norwegian flags, tinsel and red ornaments. The dining room table place settings were the classic Porsgrund Hearts and Pine dishes. Julenisse, which were a type of Santa, were part of the table decorations.

"I love it! It's so perfectly Norwegian." She bent down to read the sign about the Rommegrot tradition. "They leave a bowl of rommegrot outside the front door for the Julenisse."

"Didn't we have that at the Lutefisk dinner?" Tristan asked.

"Yes, it was the white creamy pudding with the butter and cinnamon sprinkled over the top. I love rommegrot."

"I thought it tasted good. Very rich and probably bad for the heart, though."

Annika laughed. "Good thing you're young and don't have to worry about that stuff, yet."

"Speaking of food, didn't you say they were feeding us after the tour?"

"Yes. Let's see what they're serving."

They took the elevator down to the dining area. This event was by invitation only, so there were only a couple hundred people in attendance. Tables filled with open faced sandwiches, Nordic pastries and beverages—Glögg and Aquavit—were scattered around the room. Red ribbons and greenery lavishly adorned them.

Soon their plates were filled and they found a table where they could sit down. Returning to the beverage table, they filled small mugs with Glögg and shot glasses with Aquavit.

"So what is Glögg?" Tristan asked after they sat down.

"The word means burning ember. It's similar to a mulled wine which is warmed wine with spices added. Typically, the Swedes use Aquavit, Americans use Vodka and sometimes wine is used. This one is warm wine with spices." She took a sip and nodded. "It's good."

"I agree it tastes like they used wine." He picked up the shot of Aquavit and downed it in one swallow. "That's some strong stuff." He shook his head as he said it.

"Sorry, I should've warned you. I have to sip it even though I've grown up with it."

"You are very into your Nordic heritage, aren't you?"

"It's been a big part of my life. We've –my family and I- traveled there many times to visit relatives. Our family traditions were steeped in the Nordic culture. How about you?"

"Mine, not so much. My mother was German and my dad was Norwegian but third generation, so he didn't have many traditions passed down. His mother died in childbirth, so he was raised by his dad."

"I'm sorry, I didn't mean to pry. Where are your parents living now?"

"Another sad story I'm afraid. They died in a car accident when Britt and I were still in college."

"Oh...I'm so sorry. I didn't mean to ask what appears to be deeply personal questions."

"That's okay, it's not your fault. You had no idea. So, basically it's just me and Britt for my family."

"It looks like you've done well for yourself. I mean your company seems to be thriving."

"It is. Do you have plans for Thanksgiving?" he asked changing the subject.

"I'm leaving on Wednesday evening for Phoenix to spend it with my parents. Haven't seen them much this year." She would've changed the subject if he hadn't.

He nodded. "I always try to spend time in Phoenix during the winter months. It's always a great getaway. You can usually depend on warm weather down there."

"That's true. My parents were snowbirds for quite a few years.

Now they spend more like eight months there and four months here at their cabin in Brainerd."

"How long are you staying?"

"I'll be back late Saturday night."

It appeared the conversation was over as she watched Tristan get up from the table to leave. She was sorry she'd asked about his parents. The hurt and pain she saw in his eyes at that moment spoke volumes regarding how much he must've cared about them.

"I think it's time to go. It looks like they're ready to close up." He nodded toward the empty tables around them.

Putting her coat on, she picked up her purse, pulling the key out to start her SUV. "You're right. I guess I lost track of time."

He held his hand out and she took it as they walked out to the parking lot.

"Thanks for inviting me," Tristan said stopping alongside her SUV. "I've enjoyed spending the evening with you. You are one special lady."

The moment seemed perfect for a goodnight kiss, but he remained the gentleman and backed away.

"I'll check in with you next week about the Lutsen trip before I leave for Phoenix."

He nodded and walked away.

What had just happened? Tristan had become more of a real person with actual feelings instead of a business client. Sadly, his parents were gone due to a tragic accident and the only family he had left was his sister. He had no obligation to attend the evenings' event with her, but he had. Maybe he considered her more than a business acquaintance? Now, she only needed to figure out how she would feel about their relationship being more and ultimately, her feelings toward him.

Before she knew it, Wednesday had arrived and she was at the airport waiting to board her plane to Phoenix. Her conversation with Tristan yesterday had been brief. Everything was in place for the Lutsen Ski trip, which was almost sold out. She'd agreed to lead the ski tour, but she wasn't sure exactly why she was going when she could so easily have someone else go. *Maybe because it seemed to be the perfect excuse to spend more time with Tristan.* Thankfully, when she'd informed him she would be the tour guide for the ski trip, he seemed happy she'd be joining his group in Lutsen.

The ride from the airport to her parents' house was short and before she knew it, they were all relaxing in the family room. She wasn't sure how the conversation ended up on her love life, but that's where it went.

"Honey, anything different as far as a new man?" her mom asked.

"I think that's my cue to leave, so you two can have some girl talk. I'll take the dog for a walk." Her dad picked up the leash, whistled for Brandy, their Lhasa Apso dog, and quickly left.

"I guess he wanted a way out of this conversation." She couldn't help noticing the smile on her mother's face.

"So spill."

"I told you about the *No Men for a Year* bet I made with the girls, right?"

"Yes."

"Wouldn't you know it, now I meet two men who are extremely interesting." Annika couldn't help smiling at her mother.

"Of course. I knew it. You just have to stop looking and then it will happen naturally. So who are they? Tell me about them."

"They're both exceptionally good looking, intelligent business-man. Matt is a writer for a Minnesota magazine and Tristan owns Minnesota Events and Adventures."

"Wow! Looks like you may have finally met some potential husband material."

"Not so sure about that. Remember, I made an agreement with the girls. Matt is ... nice, I think. Tristan is a great guy but he's a client of mine and there's a saying to not mix business and pleasure."

"Oh, I see. Why aren't you sure about Matt?"

"He seems like a ladies man, so not sure that would work out."

"Makes sense. And if Tristan wasn't a client, would you go out with him?" her mother asked.

"We kind of had a few business events we attended together." Annika hesitated to say more.

"And?"

"I think we got along. But what if we go out and it doesn't work, I'll lose a big client."

"If you don't, you'll always wonder."

"Wonder what?" her dad asked. "Did I come back to soon?"

"No, it's been a long day and I'm tired. I'm going to get some sleep. See you in the morning. What time is the reservation?"

"One o'clock."

The Scottsdale Princess Golf Club's Thanksgiving Buffet was one of the largest in town and the food was outstanding. Black Friday's shopping was certainly different than in Minnesota where it was freezing outside. In Arizona, the weather was in the mid-seventies and she enjoyed every minute of walking around outside while shopping with her mother. The afternoon was spent relaxing by the pool. Then before she knew it, her plane was taxiing to the gate at the Minneapolis airport.

15

"Britt, can you send Annika an invite to our Christmas Bash?" Tristan asked as he hovered over his sister's shoulder.

"Took care of that on Monday and she already accepted."

"Well, aren't you efficient?"

"That's why I get paid the big bucks." Britt smirked. "What's up with you two anyway? Are you dating?"

"We're doing business together, that's all."

"Right. Who are you kidding? Yourself? Not me that's for sure. You like her."

Tristan stared blankly out the window thinking about Annika. It started out with him just trying to keep her occupied so Matt couldn't take over and break her heart. Then....

"Tristan?" Britt asked.

"Yes?"

"Yes, you like her?"

"Of course I do. What's not to like?" Tristan asked.

"I thought you were just trying to keep her out of Matt's hands?"

"I am."

"Seems like you've been spending quite a bit of time with her since you two first met."

"I know. That's the problem. The more time I spend with her, the more I like her."

"I think she's just your type. Attractive, smart and sexy. I do think her company is a great match for us and our tour events, so I don't want you to screw the business relationship up."

"Exactly! What if we give it a go and it doesn't work? Can we still work together?" he asked.

"It would be a bit uncomfortable, but I could handle the business side and she could set us up with someone else from her office to work with."

"That might work."

"I say if you really like her and have chemistry, go for it." Britt flashed Tristan a huge smile.

"Don't forget, Matt's still in the picture. What if she picks him over me?"

"Well, that would suck big time. Especially, the second time around. I know you haven't lowered your guard and let anyone near your heart since Tonya, but it's probably time to give it a shot again."

"I do like her and trust me... chemistry isn't a problem."

"I figured that. It's kind of late, but you should see if she's busy this weekend."

"Any suggestions on what's going on in town this weekend, Sis?"

"Union Station in downtown St. Paul has a European Christmas Market and the Holiday Train. Plenty of places to have dinner around there afterwards."

"Thanks, but that's enough about my personal life. Get to work." Tristan grinned at Britt and headed to his office.

Now, the question was whether to call her or send her an email?

16

The Lutsen trip filled up rapidly, which was unexpected to say the least for a last minute tour and so close to Christmas. Tristan's membership really stepped up like he'd said they would. Unexpectedly, she'd received an invite to Events and Adventures Christmas Bash from Britt. Nordic Travel and Tours' small Christmas party was the only one on her calendar this year. With her parent's gone for the winter and a lot of companies foregoing them recently, she'd accepted. She looked forward to attending and seeing Tristan.

It was already midweek and her day was flying by when her cell phone rang. She looked down at it on her desk to see who it was. Tristan's name flashed on the screen. She quickly tapped the phone to answer. "Hello."

"It's Tristan. Hope I haven't caught you at a bad time."

"No. Just finishing up at the office."

"I know it's rather short notice, but Britt mentioned there is a European Christmas Market at Union Station along with a Holiday Train this weekend. I know it's not Nordic, actually it looks like it's mainly German, but it looks interesting. Would you be interested in checking it out Saturday afternoon and then we could find a nearby restaurant to have dinner?"

"You know I have a great-grandmother who came from Germany."

"Then by all means, you need to go."

"It sounds like fun, I'd love to join you and check it out."

"Great. Do you want me to pick you up, so we don't have to find parking for both of our vehicles?"

Annika hesitated for just a moment. "That makes sense. I'll text you my address. Three o'clock then?"

"I'll see you then."

"Bye."

It appeared she had a date with her client on Saturday. She sincerely hoped this wouldn't end up being a huge mistake. The last time someone asked her out on a date, had to have been at least a couple of years ago. Well, that was if she didn't count attending Matt's business events and she really didn't want to because they really weren't dates.

By noon on Saturday, the snow started falling and the temps fell just below freezing. It wasn't going to be warm, which was obvious by the snow flurries. She dressed in her flannel lined jeans and piled on layers, which was the best way to keep warm if you were spending time outside. Fancy boots would not work for this date, so she picked a pair of practical, warm and good walking boots. She laid out her longer mid-calf down coat and a light weight small purse.

When she saw him pull up in her driveway, she felt butterflies in her stomach. Definitely, her nerves were getting the best of her. It was just a date, not like they were even anywhere near becoming romantically involved, yet. Well, except for the one kiss, which hadn't happened again. She wasn't sure how she felt about that either.

The doorbell rang.

She opened the door and let him in. "Hello. I just need to put on my coat and grab my purse."

"No, problem. You have a nice place," he said looking around. "I didn't expect you to have a house. Thought you were more of a condo or townhouse type."

"The smaller houses and townhouses in this development were around the same price, so I decided on the house. They offer the snow removal and lawn care as a service for the home owners, too."

"That's a nice option."

"I'm ready," she said and they walked out to his black Suburban.

He opened the door for her to get in. "Luckily, the snow isn't really sticking to the roads yet. But even if does we don't have to worry, this SUV goes through anything," he reassured her.

"I heard on the news the train stops at the St. Paul Union Station around six and puts on a mini concert." She buckled her seat belt.

"Yes, according to what I read online there will be three singers. One is Kelly Prescott. Her parents were in the music business and they traveled across the U.S. performing country music so her music was influenced by that, but has a twist of being part contemporary rock, also. I listened to her new song, Church, and liked it. You'll have to let me know what you think after her performance tonight."

Twenty minutes later, they were parking in the Union Station's parking ramp which was almost full. It appeared a lot of people decided to take in the activity, also.

The marketplace consisted of small wooden structures which were separate stores with open fronts where the crafters could sell their wares. Food vendors were selling hot drinks and foods, also. It definitely felt like Christmas with all the Christmas trees and decorations.

Annika stopped in front of a food vendor's store as a mouthwatering aroma surrounded her. "My mom used to talk about her grandma making these."

Tristan turned to look at what the man was making. "Oh, German potato pancakes. I've tasted them when I was on a tour of Germany."

"I've never had them." She watched as the man dipped what looked like hash browns into the grease to be deep-fried.

"Well, we'll have to take care of that right now." He moved in front of the vendor's window. "We'll take two."

The man handed him each one wrapped separately in foil to keep them warm.

"Here you go," Tristan said and handed her one. "They look good and smell delicious."

She took a tentative small bite. Her face lit up. "It's wonderful."

He also took a bite. "Perfectly made. Just as I remembered them from my trip."

They finished eating quickly, then continued walking and browsing. Up ahead was the beverage tent.

"Let's check out the beverages inside," Tristan said, taking her hand and leading her inside.

"Glühwein-Mulled wine," she read the sign out loud. "Sounds interesting and warm."

Tristan walked up to the counter. "We'll take two."

They took their drinks and found a high table where they could set the drinks down.

Annika took a small sip, as it was still hot. "Oh, this is really good. And oh, so warm going down." She laughed.

"It is a bit cold out there. But definitely pretty with the light snow falling."

"Yes, it is. Thanks for inviting me. I'm having a great time. Even though I have German ancestry, I haven't been around too many German traditions. I can't wait to tell my mom I had potato pancakes and mulled wine!"

"I'm happy you agreed to come. The train should be here in about fifteen minutes, so we should make our way over to the train station."

By the time they arrived, a crowd already stood on the train platform waiting for the Holiday Train to arrive. Minutes later, they heard the train horn blowing and saw it come into view a ways down the tracks.

"The train is around 1,000 feet in length and has 14 decorated rail cars. Each car is decorated with hundreds of thousands of LED lights and holiday designs celebrating the Holiday season. Impressive isn't it?" Tristan asked.

"Wow. I have my very own tour guide."

"I did my homework, just so I could impress you."

"Well, thank you. I appreciate that." Her eyes were glued to the light show that had just rolled to a stop in front of them.

"That's a lot of lights." Tristan stood close behind her and partially put his arm around her as the crowd pressed in on them with everyone trying to get a front spot for the entertainment which was about to begin.

Each performer would perform one song and then three Christmas songs together. The second singer was Kelly Prescott performing her new song, *Church*. After the third singer, they united to sing, *Santa Claus is coming to Town* and *Jingle Bells*. By the end of the performance, everyone had joined in and the last song, *White Christmas,* resonated through the station as those uniquely shaped white snowflakes continued tumbling from the sky.

Annika reached up to wipe an escaped tear slowly rolling down her cheek.

"Everything okay?" Tristan asked.

She saw the concern on his face. "Yes. It was just so awesome to watch everyone joining in to sing a classic Christmas song written over eighty years ago. I'm kind of sentimental about stuff like that and the snow falling made it perfect."

He put his arm around her and hugged her. "It was quite stirring, I'll admit."

She pressed her head against his shoulder and breathed in deeply. Even though there were many layers of clothing between them, it felt comfortable and right. Although she wasn't sure it was appropriate yet at this point, so she moved apart from him a few inches. "Didn't you say something about dinner the other day? I'm a bit hungry."

"Me, too. One potato pancake wasn't quite enough. I know the perfect place. Follow me."

"Sounds like a plan." She took his extended hand and followed his lead through the crowd.

They made their way into Union Station to its own restaurant, Union Depot Grill and were lucky to find a couple of empty seats at the bar after two people left since there was a long waiting line for tables. Immediately after they sat down, the bartender handed them menus and they began reading them over.

"I'm going to have the Seared Salmon and a Coke," she stated when the bartender came back to take their order.

"I'll take the Steak Frites and water," Tristan said.

She took her coat off and fit it around the back of her bar stool then hung her purse on a hook under the bar. "It feels good to sit down and take off my coat."

He hung his coat on his stool, too. "Yes, it does."

After dinner, he drove her home on roads that had at least three inches of snow and hadn't been plowed yet. He walked her to her door while the snow continued falling, covering their coats.

"Thanks for inviting me, Tristan. I really enjoyed the afternoon and evening." She could feel the heat of his body through his open coat, because he stood so close. Her eyes focused on his baby blue eyes as his lips hovered near hers. She closed her eyes for just a second when she felt a light feathering from his lips, followed by gentle pressure and a long awaited second kiss. Her hand involuntarily reached inside his coat to hold on to him.

Time seemed to stop for a moment and then it was over.

"I should be going..." He cleared his throat. "I guess I'll see you at the Christmas party next weekend." Tristan looked into her eyes long and hard before turning toward his SUV and walking away.

Annika could sense his longing to stay, but his sense of propriety had won out.

17

Monday morning at the office, Britt entered Tristan's office with a frustrated look on her face. "How was your date?"

"We had a nice time. But you don't look too happy. What's up?" he asked.

"Matt just registered for the Christmas Bash."

"Damn! He just won't go away, will he?"

"Doesn't appear he's giving up too easily. Do you think he's still trying to get to Annika?"

"Of course, he is. He saw her spending time with me during the Hostfest Tour and wants to cause trouble for me. Again!"

"What should we do?" Britt asked.

"Can you tell him we're full?"

"That'd be nice, but he already registered online. Besides, we have room for more people and we need them to be able to register on the website."

"This is ridiculous to have to put up with him and his games again, after all these years."

"It almost appears he's trying to get even with you. He ruined your wedding and ran off with Tonya. Basically, he's already won. It just doesn't make any sense."

"Exactly!"

"All our staff will be there, so I'll just run interference for you by occupying all his time, so he can't bother you and Annika."

"That might work. I appreciate the help, Britt."

"Okay. Well, I'm going to get back to work on our Christmas Bash." Britt walked out of his office.

He'd had a great time with Annika. They were a perfect match for each other. He was sure of it, but didn't have any idea how she felt except for the fact she'd been extremely receptive to his kiss. Unfortunately, he'd been hesitant to press her further. She probably worried about their business relationship and how a personal relationship would affect it. Annika was a striking woman and he enjoyed spending time with her. They needed to have a talk about where they were going next with their relationship and it should to be soon. Definitely before Matt tried to weasel his way into her life any more than he already had.

Annika stopped at the Mall on her way home from work on Thursday night to look for a dress to wear to the Christmas Bash on Saturday night. It had been a good thing she'd checked the invitation. Dressy was noted at the bottom. She hadn't been to a dressy event for quite a while and this one was special because Tristan would be there. She wanted to look her best for him because she liked him. *A lot.* The red shimmery sateen dress she'd found was perfect and the red pair of heels in her closet matched perfectly.

Saturday evening, Annika arrived at the Hyatt Hotel near the airport where the Christmas Bash was being held in the midst of what appeared to be an overwhelmed valet service, included with the invitation, apparently for everyone attending. Typically, she didn't make use of valets but it was cold outside and she was wearing heels so it made perfect sense to use it tonight, thus she waited in line with the other cars.

To her surprise, she watched Matt get out of a vehicle at the front of the line. She wasn't sure how she felt about him being there. He seemed nice enough but probably wasn't who she needed in her life, especially with his roving eye. He headed toward the door alone, but it was obvious he was checking out all the ladies on his way. He was single, so it was probably a normal reaction to so many attractive and available ladies. Regardless, she felt relieved he would already be inside by the time she pulled up to the valet area.

As soon as she walked through the doors, she spotted Tristan near the check-in table. First, she needed to drop her coat off at the coat check.

Tristan waited for her to turn around before greeting her, as he'd made his way over to where she stood. "Annika, you look stunning." His smile was contagious.

"Thank you." He cleaned up so nice, she really wanted to close the small distance between them to give him a kiss. But it probably wouldn't be appropriate, so she held back.

He held out his hand and she took it. "Let me show you to our reserved table."

"The decorations are outstanding, Tristan. It definitely feels like Christmas in here." She noticed the numerous Christmas trees around the ballroom, all elegantly decorated. Large Christmas wreaths with red satin bows adorned the walls. The tables were covered with silver table cloths and on the centerpieces were red and silver candles intertwined with red ribbons and spruce branches, placed on mirrors.

"Mostly, it's the hotel's doing, but Britt always checks out what the hotels offer for the decorations at Christmas time before she chooses a location. She said I'd be pleased with these and I am and I'm glad you are, too. So, first stop is the bar. What would you like to drink?" he asked.

She scanned the menu listing some fun Christmas themed drinks. Christmas Snowball, Candy Cane Martini and Berry Christmas Sangria for cold drinks. Peppermint Hot chocolate, Hot buttered Rum and Egg Nog Delight along with a full bar. "I have no idea what's in the Christmas Snowball, but I'll give it a try."

"One Christmas Snowball for the lady and I'll have a Holiday Spice Bourbon."

The bartender turned to make their drinks. "Coming right up."

Annika followed Tristan to their table and sat down. She was eager to taste her drink and took a sip. "Wow, this is good. How is yours?"

"Basically a spiced up version of Bourbon. Do you want to taste it?" he asked.

"Sure." She took a sip. "I like the flavor the spices give it. Do you want to taste my Snowball?"

Tristan took a drink from the glass she handed him. "Strong coconut taste, but it's good."

"Looks like you have a great turnout tonight." Annika glanced around the room.

"It's usually our biggest event of the year. I'm glad you came."

"Thanks for inviting me. It's fun to get all dressed up at Christmas time."

"We try to make it a fun night for our members to interact with each other. There are various games set up in here and down in the hallways. Bean bag toss, Christmas trivia games, the band plays dance music and there will be Christmas song sing-a-longs. Everyone gets a Christmas gift bag when they leave, too. We have many members who live alone and don't have any family in the Twin Cities, which means they are alone on Christmas. This way, they have at least one gift to open and some treats like a box of gourmet hot chocolate packets, Christmas chocolates and new this year is a bag of gourmet popcorn drizzled with chocolate. A single serve red wine bottle is handed out with each Christmas bag."

"Wow. It really sounds like you care about your members. I'd imagine you get quite a few romantic matches from these parties. Engagements and weddings, too?"

"We do, but we don't promote the group that way because not everyone finds someone and sometimes, it just takes a while for the right person to show up and meet their special person."

"With all these eligible women in here, I'm surprised someone hasn't snatched you up already."

"It's a difficult position to be in as the owner. You'd be surprised at how many of them want to go out with me just because they think as the owner, I'm loaded."

"I'm sure you are well off. This business appears to be a lucrative one."

"Probably, if I put the time into it, I could find someone, but I think I may have already found someone who interests me."

"Oh...Is she here tonight?" Worry rose up inside her.

"She is sitting across from me right now. I assume for her, it could be a difficult position to be in. Dating a business client."

"I don't know what to say." Annika rubbed her hands together which she did when she became nervous about a situation.

"I think you are absolutely gorgeous and I've enjoyed all the time we've spent together so far. I like your adventurous nature which is apparent by all the traveling you've done. And I'm intrigued by your Norwegian interests."

"What are you saying exactly?"

"I'd like to spend more time together and see where it goes."

Finally, a smile spread over her lips. "I'd like that."

He reached across the table to hold her hand.

Only seconds later, Matt walked up to where they sat. Tristan released her hand.

"Hi. Great party, Tristan. Glad I came. Britt was nice enough to show me around and make some introductions." He looked at Annika and then Tristan.

Tristan stood up and walked around the table and Matt. He reached for Annika's hand, then looked directly at Matt. "Thrilled you're having a nice time, but we were just about to hit the dance floor. See you around."

She stood and followed him to the dance floor, where he took her in his arms for a slow dance to, *All I Want for Christmas is You.*

Wrapped in his arms felt right. His heart beat strongly against her body. Tristan had just confessed his feelings to her. She hadn't felt needed or desired in way too long. They danced and laughed, even joined in the sing-a-long to old Christmas favorites everyone knew the words to. They made it to all the games, playing along with the members who all seemed to be having a great time, too.

Once, she saw Matt attempting to join them again, but he was quickly distracted by Britt and pulled off to try a different game. Annika wasn't sure what was going on between Matt and Tristan. And Britt for that matter. All she knew was that she was falling in love with Tristan. She'd never felt like she had much in common with Matt and didn't feel attracted to him like she was to Tristan.

It was late when Tristan escorted her to the valet to get her SUV. Most of the members had already left, so the lobby was mostly deserted. They'd barely stopped near the entrance doors when she found herself wrapped in his arms.

"Did you have a good time?" His cheek was next to hers as he whispered in her ear.

"Yes, thank you." She smiled looking directly into his eyes.

Tristan gently tipped her chin up and kissed her lips with an intensity that spoke volumes about his feelings for her. Annika responded and kissed him back. Moments later, he released her and looked outside to see her vehicle had been pulled up with the valet patiently waiting. He walked her outside to her SUV. "I'll call you tomorrow."

She got in and looked up at him with a smile on her face. "I'd like that."

Tristan closed the door and waited as she drove away. A grin spread across his face as he briskly walked back into the hotel lobby, passing Matt on his way.

18

T he Nordic Travel and Tours Christmas party was on Wednesday and was all set. Holly would be attending and bringing her baby. The party would be held at the office in the conference room and the food was being catered for her small group of twenty dedicated employees. The food would have a Nordic theme consisting of Swedish Meatballs and pork ribs, baby red potatoes, Brussel sprouts, dinner rolls. For dessert, they were serving a traditional Almond rice pudding with a raspberry topping. The employees would each receive a Christmas bonus and a small wooden Julenisse, a Nordic version of Santa, she'd specially ordered from Norway.

It had been a busy week, while the whole office went over all the plans regarding the Lutsen trip. She needed the whole thing to be perfect since the bus would be leaving for Lutsen early Saturday morning. Everything was set for the company Christmas party and she was looking forward to seeing Holly and her baby.

Her phone rang and Tristan's name appeared. "Hello."

"How's your week going?" he asked.

"I think we have everything set for Lutsen."

"That's great. I'm looking forward to spending the weekend at Lutsen. And with you."

"So, I'm assuming you're a good skier?" she asked.

"Let's just say, I wouldn't have a problem with any of Lutsen's hills."

"Okay, well then you should be able to keep up with me." She laughed.

"You're on!"

"I did want to mention though that I've been watching the weather reports and they are predicting a big snowstorm, possibly a blizzard which could impact the trip."

"Snowed in at Lutsen in a blizzard? Sounds like a good time. What better place to be in a snowstorm than a mountain lodge at a ski resort?"

"I agree. But will your members agree?"

"Like I mentioned before, most of the people who signed up for the trip have no place to be on Christmas, thus they will be spending it alone, so a few extra days with other people will just be an added bonus. I wouldn't worry about it, at all."

"Well, let's hope we don't get a blizzard in case anyone *wants* to be home for Christmas."

"Sorry, I'm hoping for one now, so I can spend more time with you. I'll let you go and I'll call you Friday with our final count. And an updated weather forecast." Tristan laughed.

"Talk to you Friday," she said and disconnected the call.

On Wednesday, Holly walked through the front door with her baby in tow.

"Holly, so glad you could make it." Annika walked up to greet her with a big hug and then bent down to look at the baby in its carrier. "My you've grown," she said to the baby. "Come on into the conference room, we have everything set up for the party."

Holly followed Annika down the hall. A few of the employees

already had made their way to the room and were excited to see Holly and the baby. Soon, the office shut down for the day and everyone crowded into the conference room where the caterers had the food set up. The food buffet table looked inviting and delicious.

Annika was coerced into starting the food line and finally gave in filling her plate with the various Nordic dishes.

After eating, she looked around the room at all her dear employees who meant the world to her at Nordic Travel and Tours. They were all dedicated and extremely hard workers who had ties to the Nordic countries either by heritage, marriage or a sheer love for traveling to them. Every single one had traveled at least once to one of the countries and for most, it had been multiple times.

"Annika, I have to ask about our big new account with Events and Adventures. How's it going?" Holly asked.

Annika couldn't help chuckling a little. "Great. But I think you really meant with Tristan."

"Well, that, too."

"Really good. Even though you know my feelings about dating a client, I'm going to give it a shot."

Holly couldn't suppress her excitement. "I just knew it would work out! I'm so happy for you. I think you two will make a great power couple."

"I do like him. We'll see what happens. You know we are both going on the Lutsen trip."

"Perfect. Now, I don't want you to show him up with your skiing skills, though. You know how guys are about being the best at everything."

"I think he actually insinuated he was an expert skier, because he said Lutsen had hills."

They both laughed. "I take it you didn't say anything about your skiing expertise?"

"Not a word. I figured he'd find out soon enough."

"What about your bet?" Holly asked.

"I'd say I pretty much lost."

"Good!" Holly applauded. Then the baby started crying so she went off to get a bottle ready.

Annika walked over to the table she'd filled with Christmas gift bags for all her employees. The company had a great year financially and she wanted to share it since she couldn't have done it without them. "If I can get everyone's attention, please. I have a gift for all of you, so if you'd please come up to the table when I call your name. Inside the bags, you'll find a Christmas bonus check and a small gift from Norway."

Her employees came up one by one to get their gift bag.

"Thank you for coming to work every day with a smile on your face to make our customers' dreams of traveling to Scandinavia and seeing our beautiful state of Minnesota along with our sister states in the Midwest. I couldn't have done it without you!" she said after the last bag was handed out.

The room filled with the sound of clapping and cheering from her extremely happy employees.

Holly stood up to make an announcement, "I just wanted to remind everyone of the Nordic Christmas tradition regarding the rice pudding. Whoever gets the almond in their dish is the one who will be married by Christmas next year. But if you are already married you will have good luck in the coming year. And yes, I did check with the caterer and they followed the tradition by putting the almond in one of the dessert dishes. So who got the almond?" No one stood up. "Has everyone finished eating their rice pudding?"

Everyone nodded except Annika. She walked over to where her dish sat untouched. As she put her spoon in, it hit something hard. She uncovered it and held it up for all to see. "It's just a tradition folks, but let's talk about it next year and we'll know if there is anything to this old Nordic tradition." Annika placed the almond covered with rice in her mouth and smiled.

❅

Friday afternoon her phone rang and Tristan's name came up. "Hello."

"Hi. The day has gotten away from me and I still have a few loose ends to take care of before I even make it out of the office, but wanted to check in with you to make sure everything is set for tomorrow."

"Britt sent over your final list. Everything is good. I got this, don't worry."

"Okay. See you bright and early tomorrow morning."

"I'll be there." She disconnected the call and laughed, but wondered what he was so worried about.

An hour later, she left the office to head home to pack for the ski trip. The weather report hadn't looked good, so she packed extra clothes, just in case they got snowed in for a few extra days. The resort had emailed her earlier to say they would have plenty of food and not to worry about them having enough rooms because if her group couldn't get out, no one would be getting in, either. They, of course, would extend the discounted room rate and would offer reasonable dinner buffets. So nothing to worry about. The lodge had been able to use some of the resort's timeshare condos for the extra twenty rooms the group needed.

The next morning, she arrived at the transit station at seven sharp just as the busses arrived. They were taking two travel coaches up to Lutsen, since Tristan's group had really stepped up and booked 100 seats, so each bus would take 50 people. The busses generally could hold 60 but on a ski trip, there needed to be extra room for the ski equipment.

Peter and Kari from the office would be joining her to help since the group was so large. She found them already set up in the waiting area of the station. Normally, they'd do the check-in outside but it was 25 degrees with a wind chill of 15 degrees, so it only made sense to be inside. Peter offered to help outside with the bag check-in though, so she took a seat next to Kari. She saw through the window that Tristan and Britt had arrived and he was headed her way. "Excuse me, Kari, but I need to talk to Tristan. I'll be right back."

"I got it, don't worry," Kari said.

Annika met him at the door. "Hi. Everything is under control here but you look a bit worried about something. Is there anything wrong?"

He motioned for her to join him outside for a moment, which she did.

"I just wanted to let you know Matt booked a seat on the trip."

"Oh. I don't understand. Is it a problem?"

"I think you noticed he was interested in you, right?"

"Well, sort of, I guess. Is that a problem?"

"No. I just didn't know if it would make you feel uncomfortable, so I wanted to let you know."

"I know you said Matt was your college roommate, but I sense there might be some bad blood between the two of you."

"It's a long story for another time. I'll let you get back to what you were doing. Which bus are you going to be riding on?"

"Lutsen One."

"Save me a seat next to yours."

"Consider it done. Does Britt want to ride with us?"

"No, put her on the other one."

"And Matt?"

"Put him on the same one as Britt." With that said, he turned and walked back to the buses.

Wow! Must be quite the bad blood between them. What could be that bad? She wondered why he'd even allowed Matt to book a seat with his company on this trip.

Promptly at nine, the busses rolled out of the Metro parking lot, with Tristan in the front seat next to Annika. Both Britt and Matt were on the other bus. She really wanted to ask Tristan about it, but knew it would probably be best if they were alone for that conversation. Not one to let something like that spoil her mood, she put it out of her mind and focused on the great time she intended to have with Tristan. If Matt had other plans for her, she'd just let him know she wasn't interested.

It appeared Tristan felt the same way as he leaned over closer to her from across the aisle, since it was quite noisy on the bus, to chat about the trip.

They would be stopping at Grand Casino Hinckley for a buffet lunch from eleven to one, which allowed time to do a little gambling, also.

The second bus was a little bit behind them which was alright since it would give them a chance to unload first and go through the buffet line. In fact, Annika and Tristan had just sat down with some of the others, when the second bus pulled in.

By the time she noticed Matt in the buffet line, they'd already finished eating and were on their way to the casino to make a donation into the slot machines. Their bus loaded first and was on the road before the second bus even began loading. So, thankfully, there weren't any interactions with Matt yet, but unfortunately she knew they were coming.

Around four, the bus pulled up to Lutsen's Eagle Ridge Resort's Lodge for check-in. Annika and Tristan went inside to check in before the mass exodus from the bus. She received her Elite Condo key and waited while Tristan checked in for his room. He also had booked an Elite Condo which included a living area with a fireplace, kitchen and deck. She'd made sure it was next door to her room.

After everyone was inside the lobby, Annika spoke to the group, "Everyone, please check in at the front desk and then take your bags to your room. You'll receive the schedule for the trip along with your lift passes and vouchers for meals and drinks from the front desk. Hopefully, I'll see you all on the slopes tomorrow morning, if I don't see you in the bar this evening."

"And please wear your nametags," Tristan added. "Remember, that's how you meet people. Have fun, drink sensibly and stay safe on the slopes. And don't forget to mingle!"

Annika and Tristan grabbed a luggage rack and headed out to the bus to pick up their luggage. They were walking back into the lobby as the second bus pulled in. She knew Kari, Peter and Britt could handle everything for their bus, so she kept walking. After passing through the second long hallway, they entered the Elite Lutsen building and found their rooms.

Tristan carried her bags inside her room first. "Wow, these are really nice," he said looking around the condo.

Annika moved over to the door leading to the deck and opened it to find a spectacular view of the ski slopes, forest and Lake Superior. "This is incredible."

Tristan walked up beside her. "I agree." He stood behind her and put his arms around her waist.

She didn't move away but lingered taking in the view. Slowly, she turned to face him. "I forgot how breathtaking the view is from up here."

He looked deep into her eyes. "It's nothing compared to what I'm looking at right now. You are incredibly beautiful." He couldn't resist anymore and gently kissed her lips.

The kiss deepened as she kissed him back.

A few minutes later, he ended the kiss. "I'm going to let you get unpacked and then hopefully, you will join me for dinner."

"Yes, I will. Afterwards, we should stop by the bar to make sure everyone is having a good time."

"Deal." Tristan and Annika walked back inside the condo.

"Six o'clock?" She nodded.

Tristan nodded back, then left to drop his bags inside his room and get cleaned up for dinner.

Kari texted Annika that the second bus was all checked in with no problems.

Annika texted back that she'd see her and Peter later in the bar.

As soon as Tristan was in his room, he saw a text from Britt. She was checked in and had the room next door. He walked over to her room and knocked.

Britt opened the door and let him in.

"So how did it go with Matt?" he asked.

"He wasn't too happy to be on my bus. He actually asked if I couldn't move someone off of your bus, so he could be on the one with Annika."

"Damn. He's going to be trouble."

"Hopefully, once he realizes Annika likes you, he'll back off."

"Didn't work last time. Back then, I was engaged and two weeks from the altar. Not a chance it's going to work this time."

"I can try to talk to Annika, if you'd like."

"Maybe, but I don't want to play that card unless we have to."

"You know Annika is a totally different person than Tonya. They have different personalities. She may not get caught up in Matt's deception."

"Let's hope so."

"You really like her, don't you?" Britt asked.

"She's a really special person. I could see spending the rest of my life with her."

"Dang! You got it bad for her."

"You wanted me to take a chance again." Tristan ran his fingers through his hair in frustration.

"I know. But do you think she feels the same way?" she asked.

"At the Christmas Bash, we talked about seeing where this mutual attraction could take us."

"Oh. Well, I don't think you have anything to worry about then."

"I just don't want to spend the whole weekend looking over my shoulder to see if Matt's going to try to interrupt us and spoil a special moment." Tristan began pacing.

"I'll try my best to keep him away from you two."

Tristan walked out and opened the door to his room so he could change clothes for dinner.

19

Eagle Landing was the lodge's four restaurant's area. Eagle Tap served brews and pizza, Eagle Buffet featured a daily themed buffet, Eagle Grill served hamburgers and sand-wiches along with breakfast in the morning and Eagle Dinner Club was fine dining at its best, complete with linen tablecloths. After checking out each restaurant's posted menu, they chose the Grill and were promptly seated.

"I can't get over this view," Tristan said while they took in the resort decorated in its Christmas finery, through the large window.

"It's like a miniature version of Vail in Colorado. The little main street lined with shops and food eateries is awesome. And all the lights! I love coming up here each year."

"Oh, so you're a regular, then?"

"If you consider once a year regular."

"Do you ski Colorado each year, too?" Tristan asked.

"Definitely! I try to rotate them and ski a different mountain each year."

"So, you've skied all Colorado has to offer?"

"Multiple times. Along with Utah and Montana's finest. How about you?" Annika asked.

"Let's just say, I've skied my fair share of hills and mountains."

Their server brought out their brews followed by the burgers and fries soon after. They noticed a few others from the tour come in the restaurant to eat, but thankfully, not Matt.

Later that evening around nine, Tristan and Annika walked into the bar which was full. It seemed like almost everyone from the tour had congregated here.

Annika spotted Britt talking with Matt and a couple of other women. Upon a closer look, she recognized the women from the Hostfest tour. Maybe they would be able to occupy Matt's time, so she wouldn't have to deal with him?

It was Saturday night, after all, so there were quite a few locals who'd also stopped in to drink and listen to the local band, *Toppers*, play.

Once the music started, it became very loud and difficult to carry on a conversation.

Kari and Peter stopped over to chat for a few minutes before moving on to work the crowd.

Annika and Tristan were standing next to a high-top table where their brews sat on paper coasters.

Suddenly, Matt was beside her, standing much to close for her comfort level. "Hi, how have you been?" he asked.

"Fine. What made you decide to join the tour?" she asked as point blank as she could be.

"Sounded fun and thought maybe we could spend some time together?" Matt stated calmly.

Tristan looked directly at Matt, but didn't say a word.

They both waited for Annika's reply.

"Matt, I'm sorry but I'm working and will be busy making sure everything on this tour flows smoothly. Tristan and I will be overseeing the tour. I did see your friends from the Hostfest tour, Sue and Tara, they might be interested in occupying your time up here."

"I see. You and Tristan it is?" Matt leered daggers at Tristan.

"Matt, here you are. I've been looking all over for you." Britt walked up, looped her arm through Matt's, and led him off. "I have some ideas for your article."

"She is good!" Annika watched them walk away, deep in conversation.

"Dang good!" Tristan chuckled. "Do you want to get out of here?"

"Thought you'd never ask." She took his offered hand as they slipped out of the bar and down the hall leading to their condos.

"Would you like to join me in my condo for a glass of wine and a roaring fire?" Tristan asked.

"Sounds perfect."

Immediately after they entered his condo, he turned the gas fire place on, took out a bottle of wine from the refrigerator, and poured two glasses.

Annika sat down on the couch in front of the fireplace.

He sat down next her and tipped his glass against hers in a toast. "Here's to a great first day of the ski trip."

"So far, so good," she said.

"Are you worried about something?"

"No. I was just looking forward to us getting know each other better, but it seems like Matt is always popping up unexpectedly to interrupt us." Annika took another sip of wine.

"We'll just have to make sure he's busy elsewhere, so we can have some quality time together."

"Not sure if that will work," Annika stated.

"Matt likes to be surrounded by women. It appears Sue and Tara will try to occupy his time. And if that doesn't work Britt will keep him busy."

"Okay, let's hope it works. If not, maybe I'll just have to have a little talk with him."

"Probably should wait a little bit first and see how it goes. Enough about him. Let's talk about us. What would you like to know about me?" Tristan asked.

"What are your thoughts about marriage and children?" she asked.

"Wow. You certainly are forthright with your questions. When I find the right person for me, I probably wouldn't waste a lot of time dating, I'd want to get married and start a family soon. After all, we're not getting any younger. What are your thoughts on the subject?"

"Oh, I definitely want to get married and have children." She locked eyes with Tristan. The air was filled with electricity from the chemistry between them. She took a sip of wine and set the glass down on the coffee table.

"Seems we are in complete agreement." He held her gaze, took way more than a sip of wine, more like a gulp, and set his glass down. The lights were dim and they were bathed in the firelight. He gently pulled her toward him and kissed her.

Annika's head was swimming in ecstasy from the feel of his lips on hers. It felt so wonderful encircled in his arms and was a place she'd like to stay forever. She kissed him back completely and anticipated what their future could be.

The doorbell rang.

"Tristan, are you in there?" Britt asked from outside the door.

"Just a minute," he replied still holding Annika in his arms.

"Guess that's my queue to get going to my condo. It's late and we need to be up early to hit the slopes." She stood up and walked to the door.

"What time are we heading out?"

"I'm going to have a light breakfast at eight and hope to be on the slopes by nine."

"I'll pick you up at eight, then," he said and leaned in for a quick kiss good night.

She laughed. "I'm right next door."

He opened the door to see Britt waiting with a huge smile.

She walked in after Annika walked out. "Annika, see you tomorrow, too." Britt said.

Annika waved at her, then opened her door and walked in as the door closed behind her. Since no one could see her, she did a silent happy dance! Love was definitely knocking on her door and she welcomed it completely.

20

Sunday morning proved to be a bright sun-shiny type of day, obviously the calm before the storm as a blizzard was on its way. By nine, Tristan and Annika were waiting in line for the gondola to take them to the top of Lutsen Mountain. It wasn't crowded yet, which was why she always made it a plan to start early. The view from the top of the mountain was even more spectacular than at the lodge. Lake Superior was partially frozen but still retained open water in the center of the immense lake. Being the largest freshwater lake in the world with the third largest volume in the world, it rarely froze over completely, but if it did, it most likely wouldn't happen until February or March. The hills of the Lutsen Mountains along with Lake Superior were covered in snow from the recent snow storms and the area was expecting at least another foot of snow in the next few days. The odds for the tour making it back to Minneapolis before the storm hit were slim.

"We really lucked out to get the whole gondola to ourselves," Tristan said as he stood next to her while taking in the view.

"Yes, we did." She graced him with a smile. "I heard the snow is pristine this morning. Can't wait to be one of the first ones to hit the Black Bear slope."

"Isn't it a blue run?"

"Yes, I haven't skied yet this winter and it's always wise to do a warm up run first. And I wasn't sure what level your skiing skills were at."

"I'm a very experienced and skilled skier. How about you?"

"Me, too. So we will start with a blue, next a black diamond and then a double black diamond, if you're up to it."

"Sounds good to me."

The gondola stopped and they exited to the snow. Once they stepped into their skies, they made sure they had their hats in place, face masks pulled up and gloves on.

"Ready?" she asked.

"Yes."

"Let's do this," Annika said and waited until Tristan took off then followed his expert turns down the hill.

At the bottom of the hill, she stopped beside him, pulled down her face mask, and gave him a look.

"What? I told you I could ski any hills or mountains." He laughed. "You know, you're pretty good yourself."

"I know." She laughed.

"I guess we'll be well suited to ski together. Another thing we have in common."

"Another?"

"Skiing and a desire for adventure." He skied over to the gondola line. "You coming? Or are you afraid of a black diamond run?"

"I love black diamonds," she said moving to get in line next to him.

Sometime after noon, they ended up in the mountain top chalet eating lunch, where they ran into Britt.

"Hi! How's the skiing going?" Britt asked.

"Great. The slopes are in perfect condition," Tristan said. "Do you want to join us for a quick lunch?"

"Please, join us," Annika said.

"Thanks." Britt sat down at their table.

"So are you an expert skier, too?" Annika asked.

"I'd say Tristan and I are at the same level." Britt smiled at her brother.

"So is Annika, from what I've seen," Tristan added.

"Great! Tristan never seems to find anyone who can keep up with him, besides me and a few of his college buddies," Britt offered.

"Where did you go to college?" Annika asked turning toward Tristan.

"I went to the University of Minnesota in Duluth. UMD. And I was on their ski team," Tristan stated with a grin.

"That explains why you're so good." Annika laughed.

"And how did you get to be such a great skier, if I may ask?" he inquired.

"I attended St. Olaf College in Northfield and was on their ski team."

"Makes sense. It's a Scandinavian college isn't it?" Tristan asked.

"Yes. And skiing is very Nordic, you know." Annika couldn't help laughing.

"Well, if anyone cares, I too, went to UMD and was on their ski team," Britt offered. "So I guess that makes all three of us excellent skiers."

"We haven't seen Matt, yet. Thought maybe he'd be with you, Britt," Annika stated.

"I offered to ski with him this morning, but he said he was joining Sue and Tara. I'm thinking by now, he is regretting it because I overheard them say they were just beginners. And since he also skied on the UMD ski team, he is going to be extremely bored." Britt smiled.

They all finished their lunches and headed back out to get some more skiing in before it got dark.

"I'm going to check on Matt and see how he's doing on the bunny hill." Britt laughed and took off down the hill in perfect slalom style.

"She is good," Annika stated.

"That's my sister. Always liked to show off her expertise on the slopes. Ready?" he asked.

Annika took off down the hill with Tristan following right behind her.

At dusk, they headed into Eagle's Landing for dinner.

"It's a pasta theme for the buffet, does that sound good to you?" Annika asked.

"Pasta works for me."

"I'm going to change out of these clothes first." Annika motioned toward her ski pants and jackets.

Tristan nodded in agreement and they walked down the halls to their condos.

A half hour later, Annika walked out of her condo to find Tristan dressed in blue jeans and a dark blue flannel shirt, leaning against the wall waiting patiently for her. He looked darn good. She'd have to be crazy to pass up this great guy who she, undeniably, had the chemistry thing going with, also.

"You look great," Tristan complimented as he held his arm out for her.

"Thanks." Annika had carefully chosen her attire. Skin tight blue jeans, neatly tucked in her black, ankle high boots and a tapered, red flannel shirt hung loosely to her hips. Her long blonde hair flowed down her back in gentle waves from the braid she'd worn earlier.

The line for the buffet was long since many from the tour had chosen the same option for dinner. She looked around and saw Matt up ahead of them in the line with Tara and Sue. Britt was at the head of the line conversing with the hostess who was giving out table assignments after collecting their dinner vouchers. Annika watched Matt turn her way and make eye contact, then start to make his way to the back of the line where she and Tristan were standing. She looked toward Tristan and saw a scowl cross his face when he, too, observed Matt trying to make eye contact.

Luckily, Britt had also been watching Matt and intercepted him quickly by drawing him into a conversation with her until he received his table number and was escorted away by the hostess.

Annika wasn't exactly sure why Britt had offered to try to keep Matt busy. She was thankful though because she hadn't been physically attracted to Matt the way she was to Tristan. Maybe Britt had dated Matt sometime in the past since it sounded like they'd all attended UMD together?

Since they'd practically wound up at the end of the line, most people had already left and made their way out to the bonfires, by the time they'd finished eating. The conversation was interesting as usual with Tristan filling her in on how his business operated and how much he enjoyed helping singles meet other singles and sometimes even their future spouses.

"Ready for dessert?" Annika asked.

"What'd you have in mind?" he asked smiling heartily her way.

"S'mores, of course! We're making them outside at the bonfire." Annika stood up ready to go. "We'll have to swing back to our rooms first to grab our jackets."

About ten minutes later, they sat on a bench next to one of the bonfires with their S'mores package filled with graham crackers, marshmallows, Hershey's chocolate candy bars, and long metal skewers. Quickly, they slid marshmallows onto the skewers, roasted them to a golden-brown color, then placed them on top of the piece of chocolate lying on the graham cracker and gently pushed the second graham cracker down on top of the marshmallow.

Tristan took a bite. "I'd forgotten how good these are. It's been a long time since I've had one."

"I love S'mores. I usually only have them in the summer, but this winter bonfire works, too." Annika took another bite.

Altogether, there were six bonfires outside the lodge, each surrounded by benches full of people. Some talking, some singing Christmas songs and many were making S'mores, too.

"Were the S'mores your idea?" he asked.

"When I plan tours, it's always all the little details that really make them memorable."

"Definitely the S'mores will be remembered along with other things." Tristan leaned closer to her and as their eyes locked, their lips came together in a kiss.

Obviously, her love life was spinning out of control, she thought.

As they walked back to their condos, she knew she no longer cared what her friends were going to say about the bet. Losing had never felt so good.

21

Annika woke to a partly cloudy morning with intermittent peaks of sun. She knew by tomorrow morning, it would be a totally different story when they would be surrounded by heavy cloud cover and snow. Lots of snow! But today would be a full day for the tour with skiing and snowmobiling.

Tristan was meeting her at the Eagle Grill for breakfast.

She decided to leave her snowmobile suit in the condo and go back for it after they ate. They'd fallen into a comfortable, more than friends routine and she was excited to see him. She walked directly over to the table where he sat. "So how are you doing this morning?" she asked.

"Can't go wrong sitting across from a beautiful woman who's also a savvy business woman." Tristan smiled at her.

"We have snowmobiles reserved for this morning and I'm looking forward to snowmobiling. How about you?" she asked.

"I love snowmobiling. I hope you have a snowmobile suit to wear." He observed her attire.

"It's back in the condo." She nodded.

They both ordered the Lutsen platter consisting of eggs, bacon, hash browns and pancakes. The one nice thing about a lot of physical activity was being able to eat a big meal.

After breakfast, she went back to her condo to change into her snowmobile suit and then walked out to the snowmobile rental building. As she reached the snowmobiles parked outside, she saw Matt talking to Tristan. When they noticed her, Matt gave her a nod and walked away.

"Everything okay?" she asked looking toward Matt's retreating back.

"Oh, Matt? He's just being his usual self, showing up where he shouldn't be."

"I'm not sure I follow?"

"Don't worry about it. Matt and I don't see eye to eye on much these days."

"Ma'am, this is yours," the attendant said standing next to a shiny red snowmobile. "Have you driven one before?"

"Yes." Annika got on and looked over the gauges. "Looks similar to the ones I've been on before."

"You, sir?" the attendant asked.

"Got it." Tristan sat down on the silver snowmobile next to Annika's.

With helmets on, they took off toward the snowmobile trails. Miles and miles of pristine snow lay ahead of them lined with majestic groves of pine trees. At the Lake Superior lookout point, they stopped to take in the incredible view and have a cup of hot chocolate for her and coffee for him from their thermoses.

"I think you've done this before," Tristan commented.

"I think you've done this before, too," she answered.

"I own a couple of snowmobiles and have been known on the spur of the moment to take a vacation day after a snowstorm to escape for a while down a trail of freshly fallen snow."

"My grandfather used to have snowmobiles. It's been awhile since I've been on one, though," Annika explained.

"You and I seem to have quite a few similar interests." Tristan put his arm around her and drew her in for a kiss. "And I really like kissing you."

"I really like you kissing me." She gave him a quick kiss, then turned and ran to her snowmobile, revved the engine and called out, "Catch me if you can!"

"Not fair, you have a head start!" Tristan jumped on his snowmobile and took off after her.

They made it back to the lodge in time for lunch at the Eagle Tavern where they split a pizza after dropping off their snowmobile suits in their condos. The bar was filled with people talking, eating and having a good time. Thankfully, she didn't see Matt.

"I have to make a few calls this afternoon, do you want to meet me for a few runs down the black diamond hills around three?" Tristan asked.

"Sure. I'm going to head out there after lunch, maybe see if Kari or Peter wants to take a couple of runs. I'll meet you at the gondola lift area at three."

Annika changed into ski gear at her condo and left Tristan in his condo to make calls.

Outside the lodge, she set her skis down to look around for Kari or Peter. Unfortunately, she didn't see either one. She'd left them each a text, but hadn't heard back from them, yet.

Matt suddenly showed up and walked over to her. "I guess I finally got lucky and found you alone. Are you available to take a run down a black diamond with me?"

Annika scanned the area and still didn't see Kari or Peter. *It wouldn't hurt to join him for one run, would it?* "Sure," she answered and got in the gondola line with him.

Once inside the gondola, he asked, "So where's Tristan?"

"Back at his condo, he had some business calls to make."

"He seems to be keeping you pretty busy," Matt said as he moved closer to Annika.

"We are working together to make sure everyone has a great time on the Lutsen tour. Are you having a good time?" she asked.

"I'd be having a better time if we could spend more time together."

"Matt, I'm sorry if you got the wrong idea, but I'd prefer to just be friends." Annika was glad there were only two other people in the gondola with them since it appeared her and Matt were going to have a private conversation that really wasn't private at all. The gondola stopped mid mountain and the other couple got out.

"Are you and Tristan just friends?"

"I don't think that's an appropriate question you should be asking me."

"I think you're wrong. I like you a lot and want to protect you from Tristan."

"Protect me? From what?" she asked.

"Getting your heart broken."

"Do you know something about Tristan I don't?"

"You seem like the type of woman who wants to get married and have a family. But trust me, that's not what Tristan is looking for."

"Why do you say that?"

"Tristan was engaged before and he called off the wedding, just two weeks prior to the date." A wicked grin crossed Matt's face.

The gondola stopped and the door opened. Matt stepped out with his skis in hand and waited for Annika to exit, also.

They both moved away from the gondola area.

"Why did he call it off?" Annika locked eyes with Matt. She needed to know if he was telling her the truth.

"He just wasn't up for spending the rest of his life with just one woman and children would get in the way of his career." Matt stepped into his skis and took off down the double black diamond with the ease of an expert skier.

Annika watched him disappear down the hill. She didn't want to believe him, but why would he lie? Just when she finally felt she had found someone who she could spend the rest of her life with, she was filled with doubt. After stepping into her skis, she flew down the hill in her perfect ski team form.

When she reached the bottom of the slope, Matt was nowhere to be found. She looked toward the lodge where the gigantic clock showed the time was a little before three. Over in the gondola area, she spotted Tristan waiting for her. The time for confrontation on the subject of his previous engagement would have to wait, because this most certainly wasn't the time or place for a private conversation. She put on her happy face and skied over to Tristan and they got in line for the gondola. This time in the gondola, there were six other people riding all the way to the top.

"You seem awfully quiet," Tristan observed.

"Oh. I'm just thinking about the snow storm coming our way. You know we most likely will not be heading home tomorrow." She only half lied.

"Probably not. Hey, but on the bright side, we'll get to spend Christmas Eve together."

They exited the gondola and Annika stepped into her skis. "Just hope everyone else will feel the same way about it. See you at the bottom." And then she took off down the hill.

Tristan caught up with her and they both came to a stop at the bottom of the hill, only minutes apart. "Want to go again?" he asked.

"I'll have to take a rain check. I need to catch up with Kari and Peter to go over the dinner event tonight."

"Okay, I'm going to go for another run. I'll see you later, then."

"I'll see you at the conference room where the dinner will be." She nodded.

"Do you want me to stop by your room on my way to dinner?"

"No. I have to be down there early, so I'll just meet you there." Annika turned and walked toward the lodge.

She knew he was watching her because she could feel his eyes piercing her back. He must be totally confused by her behavior, but she didn't want to get into a discussion that may lead to an argument with bystanders observing. Not until she reached the door did she turn to look back just in time to observe him turn away and head over to the gondola. She wanted to take another run down the black diamond but she didn't want to do it under the tense conditions she'd just created between them. She would probably regret that decision, since she may not have another chance to ski with Tristan. And it was all because of something Matt had said. Heck, she had no idea if what he'd said was even true. Her gut told her that if Tristan had called off his wedding, he had a good reason. However, the only way she would get confirmation on anything was to be forthright and just plain ask him.

Annika dropped off her skis and outerwear in her condo. She'd received a text from both Kari and Peter, both saying they were at the conference room getting the party set up. The party would be Christmas casual, so she changed into black jeans with a red, white and black shirt with a Nordic Christmas design. Then she slipped on her black, knee high boots. After she touched up her make-up and restyled her hair, she left for the conference room.

She was thankful to have two dedicated employees who'd taken care of everything already. The room looked perfect! A fully decorated Christmas tree sat in each corner of the room, the majestic fireplace sat on one wall decorated with Christmas stockings. The tables were covered in red tablecloths with gorgeous centerpieces in red, silver and gold. The room definitely said Christmas!

At about six, people had started lining up just as the waiters began bringing the food out to the buffet. On one side of the room was a band which had just finished setting up and they were playing a warm up holiday song.

"It looks like we're ready, should we begin letting people in?" Kari asked.

"Yes, certainly. Let's get this party started." Annika walked over to see who was already in line outside the doors.

She didn't see either Matt or Tristan, yet. A large part of her didn't want to talk to either one of them while another part yearned to hear a really good reason that would've prompted Tristan to call off his wedding. Actually, she had no desire at all to talk to Matt.

Just minutes later, Tristan walked in looking so darn handsome she wanted to give him a big kiss.

Apparently, he had the same idea. He walked directly up to her.

"You look beautiful," he complimented and leaned forward to give her a quick kiss. "How's everything going?"

"So far, so good."

"It certainly feels like Christmas in here."

"Thank you. I always try to deliver on my promises," she stated.

"That you have done. Can I get you a drink?" he asked.

"I'll have a Red Christmas Sangria, thank you."

"Where's our table? I'll meet you there."

"Against the back wall. The one with the reserved sign on it," she explained.

Tristan walked away. She spotted Britt walk in with Matt. She was deeply concerned about what the relation was with Matt and Britt. Did Britt actually like Matt? Or was she just trying to occupy his time, so he wouldn't bother her and Tristan? Regardless, she seemed to be with him quite often.

Ultimately, this was a Christmas party and she wanted it to be great, so she decided to forget about her conversation with Matt earlier in the day and simply have a good time with a great guy. She walked over to the table where Tristan waited for her to join him, sat down next to him and took a sip of her drink. "It looks like everyone is having a good time and the line is gone for the buffet. Do you want to get some food? I for one am hungry after all of our strenuous skiing."

"Sure," he said.

They filled their plates with the scrumptious foods in the buffet. Basically, it was a carved roast beef dinner with lots of sides to go with it.

Kari and Peter joined them and surprisingly, Britt did, also. The conversation was lively, mostly about skiing and snowmobiling.

"I see someone I want to say hello to. I'll be back," Tristan said and excused himself from the table.

Kari and Peter left to go over the song list with the band, leaving just Annika and Britt at the table.

"You seem a bit quiet and preoccupied tonight, is everything okay?" Britt asked.

Annika debated if she should say anything to Britt, but it was gnawing at her, so she decided to confide in her. "I ran into Matt this afternoon skiing and he told me some unsettling information about your brother."

By the look crossing Britt's face, it seemed she wasn't in the least bit surprised. "What did he say?" she asked.

"He said Tristan was engaged and called off the wedding two weeks beforehand."

"I don't suppose he told you why Tristan cancelled the wedding, did he?" Brit questioned.

"Not exactly. Do you know why?"

"Yes and so does Matt. What did he tell you the reason was?"

"He said Tristan isn't the marrying kind and he doesn't want to be married or have a family."

"Of course, he did." Anger was written all over Britt's face. "He would never tell you the real reason."

"Will you tell me?" Annika asked. "I really like Tristan and he told me he wanted to get married and start a family. If he really doesn't, I'm not interested in continuing our relationship."

"I could but you need to ask Tristan and when you do, believe what he tells you. Matt is a liar and a manipulator. He will use any methods available to get what he wants. That is why Tristan and Matt aren't friends anymore. The bad blood between them is for a good reason. Trust is important in a relationship. You need to talk to Tristan."

"Wow. Sounds like something big happened between them to cause this if they used to be best friends. But if that's so, why have you been hanging around with him?"

"You know the old saying, 'Keep your enemies close'? Well, that's what I've been trying to do. He writes for a very prominent magazine in Minnesota and we don't want him to damage our company's reputation that we've worked so hard to build, so we've been trying to play nice with him."

"Oh, I was beginning to think you and Matt were a thing."

"That's a definite no. I wouldn't wish him on my worst enemy. He is bad news which is why I've been trying to keep him away from you. I've heard what he was like in college. From what I heard, he only likes the chase, if you catch my meaning. Promise me you'll talk to Tristan. He likes you a lot, too."

"Okay. I'll go look for him now." Annika left the table in search of Tristan. She was in a much better mood now, thanks to Britt.

She became sidetracked talking to some of the tour members and didn't see Matt come up behind her. "The Christmas event has turned out well. Everyone seems to be having a great time."

"Yes, they do. Thank you."

"Would you care to dance with me?"

"Actually, I promised the next dance to Tristan." Annika turned and walked away. Luckily, she spotted Tristan coming toward her.

"Everything okay?" he asked scowling at Matt.

"Yes, now it is. I think this dance is yours."

Tristan led her to the dance floor where he took her in his arms. She leaned her head against his shoulder and immediately felt immensely calmer. The heat from his body warmed her and the chemistry between them ignited. They were made for each other. She knew it for sure at that moment and she was sure the reason he had for calling off his wedding was a legitimate and warranted one. She looked up into his glazed eyes and kissed him. Not a quick light kiss but a long passionate kiss.

When the kiss ended, he whispered in her ear, "I think we need to talk."

"Yes, we do." She took his hand and followed him out of the room. They walked silently down the hallways leading to their condos.

22

Annika sat down on the sofa and Tristan sat down next to her.

"Tell me what's going on. You seemed a little mad at me earlier but then you just kissed me in front of a room full of people. Don't get me wrong the kiss was a surprise and the feeling was mutual. And you can kiss me anytime you want."

She leaned over and kissed him again, then leaned back on the sofa, so she could look into his eyes. "Were you engaged to someone, but called off the wedding?"

"Oh...Who told you that?"

"Matt."

"Of course, he would. I'm assuming he didn't tell you why?"

"No. Well, not really."

"Let me make this short and to the point. I caught him in bed with my fiancé two weeks before the wedding."

Annika felt the color drain from her face. "That's horrible."

"Exactly. I couldn't believe she would betray me with my so-called *best friend* at the time. Best friends simply don't do that, either. So for me, it was a double betrayal. I called off the wedding and have barely spoken to either one of them since that devastating night until he showed up in town recently. I was trying to *play nice* so he wouldn't write a bad article about my company or yours in his magazine."

"What is he trying to accomplish?"

"He is bad news when it comes to women. His policy is love 'em and leave 'em. I heard he broke up with my fiancé a few months after I caught them together. She actually had the gall to call me then and ask me to take her back because she still loved me. I told her flat-out no. Trust is one of the most important parts of a relationship, next to love."

"I, actually, sort of went out with him a couple of times, but there was no chemistry at all. I mainly went because I didn't want him to write a bad article about my company, either. Then when Britt kept spending time with him, I thought she liked him."

"Not a chance. When she met you, she liked you and told me we would make a perfect power couple," Tristan explained. "Her spending time with him was her way of allowing you and me to get to know each other better by us spending time together."

"Oh. I guess it worked."

"Initially, I wasn't too excited about starting a relationship with anyone to be honest. I went along with her plan to spend time with you in order to save you from Matt, but the more time I spent with you, the more I liked you."

"Me, too. I wasn't looking for a relationship either, plus I kept telling myself not to get involved because you were my business client. I have this silly rule about not mixing business with pleasure. Unfortunately or fortunately, depending on how you look at it, the more time I spent with you, the more I liked you."

"Then, I guess this time Matt will come out the loser."

"But I don't understand why he told me about the wedding being called off? He must've known I'd find out the truth?" she asked.

"He wanted to create doubt in your mind about me because he must've already known he hadn't succeeded in his pursuit of you. Did you say anything to him that would make him believe you weren't interested in him?" Tristan asked.

"I told Matt, I just considered him a friend."

"Good for you. I'm glad you came to that conclusion on your own."

"What do we need to do about him?"

"We'll figure that out tomorrow."

"You do want to get married and start a family, right?"

"Are you proposing?" He chuckled and gave her a light kiss.

"Matt said you didn't."

"Yes, I want to get married and start a family, but I think we should give it a few more months before I give you a real proposal and we set a wedding date."

"It's a deal!" Annika moved closer, wrapped her arms around his neck, and kissed him.

Tristan puller her closer and kissed her back.

They fell asleep wrapped in each other's arms on the sofa.

About midnight, they woke and decided the bed in the loft bedroom would be more comfortable. Through the open curtains of the patio door leading to a small upper level deck, the snow could be seen falling heavily with perfectly designed sparkling snowflakes.

Annika took off her boots and laid down on the bed next to Tristan. He wrapped his arms around her. Soon, they fell asleep watching the snow falling on top of the three inches already on the ground.

They woke the next morning around eight to a barrage of text messages beeping on their phones. It was as they'd suspected, they were snowed in at Lutsen. The plows wouldn't be able to get out to even get started clearing the roads until it stopped snowing. A foot of snow was already on the ground and still furiously fell from the sky.

Annika went back to her room to shower and change. The lodge left a message stating the buffet was open as planned and for her to stop at the lobby desk when she came down for breakfast. She returned texts to Kari and Peter telling them to begin executing plan B and she would meet them at the buffet at nine.

Tristan and Annika walked into the Eagles Buffet holding hands.

Britt, Kari and Peter were already seated and smiled as they walked up to the table and sat down.

"It looks like you two worked everything out," Britt stated.

"You would be correct," Tristan answered.

Both Kari and Peter displayed huge grins.

"We already talked to the front desk," Kari stated. "And they have extended all the rooms for an extra night at half price. Since it's Christmas Eve, they'll serve Christmas dinner in the same conference room we were in last night. One of the staff is actually their part time DJ, so he will make sure Christmas music is playing all night. They will try to get the blue hill open by one, so anyone who wants to ski can. The ice rink will be cleared also for skating. The snowmobiles will not be available due to the decreased visibility on the trails."

"Wow, you've been busy. Thank you for executing plan B." Annika smiled at the both of them.

After they finished breakfast, everyone was engaged in lively conversation when Matt walked up to the table. "So we're snowed in," he commented.

"Yes," Tristan answered as he took Annika's hand in his on the table.

Matt's eyes fixated on their hands. "So...happy, everything worked out for you and Annika," he managed to surmise.

"Anything else you needed?" Tristan asked.

"No, that's all I needed to know."

Britt got up from her chair and took Matt by the arm. "I wanted to check in with you on the article you're writing." She led him out of the restaurant.

Tristan, Annika, Kari and Peter, all burst out laughing as soon as Matt and Britt were out of their view.

The rest of the afternoon, Tristan and Annika had a blast skiing the blue hill in the blizzard and later went ice skating which proved to be fun even though they had to keep shoveling the snow off the ice.

For dinner, everyone met in the conference room for a traditional turkey and meatball dinner with all the fixings. After dinner, the DJ played both old and new Christmas music which everyone could sing along to. They danced and stopped under the mistletoe for magical Christmas kisses.

Tristan and Annika in particular stopped often under the many mistletoe spots. They spotted Matt doing the same, only with different ladies each time.

Around eleven that evening, Annika and Tristan, walked back to their condos.

"Mine or yours?" she asked.

"Mine. I have a Christmas gift for you," he answered with a sly smile.

"Oh... But I didn't get one for you."

"Just having you here with me is all I could ask for." He opened the door and took her hand to lead her inside. Once the door closed, he took her in his arms and kissed her. He looked deeply into her eyes. "I think I may very well be falling in love with you, Annika."

"Me, too," she said and kissed him. Then she pulled away and laughed. "I mean with you, not with myself."

He chuckled as he shook his head. "Have a seat. I'll pour us some wine."

Annika sat down and picked up the TV remote. She turned on a Christmas music station.

Tristan set two glasses of wine on the coffee table. He left and returned moments later with a wrapped present. It was a tiny box. "Go ahead and open it." He handed it to her.

"You really shouldn't have..."

"Open it."

Annika opened it to find the Viking necklace she'd almost bought at Hostfest. She gasped. "I really wanted this necklace. Thank you."

"You're welcome. When I saw how much you liked it, yet you walked away, I lingered till you were out of sight and bought it for you. I thought it would make a perfect Christmas gift."

"I really think I'm falling in love with you," Annika confessed.

Tristan took her in his arms and kissed her.

This time, as they lay on his bed looking out the window, the sky was clear with the moon shining down on the pristine newly fallen snow.

23

Christmas Day morning, the Eagle Landing restaurants were filled to capacity with all the Events and Adventure tour members, having their last meal before leaving for Minneapolis.

The buses rolled out of Lutsen at eleven sharp. Annika and Tristan were on one bus and Britt was on the other bus to keep an eye on Matt. The buses didn't stop on the drive back to Minneapolis, since a few members did have families they needed to make appearances at for Christmas gatherings. They made it back by five which was a day late, but better late than never, as the saying goes.

Tristan took her hand. "I know you are leaving tomorrow morning for Phoenix and need to pack, so I'll just give you call around nine."

"That'll work." Annika smiled as Tristan took her in his arms for a goodbye kiss.

"I guess, I'll see you when you get back on New Year's Day," he said and watched her leave.

Britt walked up to stand next to him. "Did you tell her you have a house in Phoenix?"

"No," Tristan answered with a sly grin.

"You're planning on getting a ticket to go down there, right?"

"Should I?" he joked.

"Of course, you should. Probably should let her have at least one day alone with her parents, first though."

"I can do that. The ticket will probably be cheaper, too." Tristan couldn't hold back the laughter.

"So you think this is funny," she began laughing with him.

"Seriously though, when should I tell her I have a house in Scottsdale?"

"Not till you get down there, at least."

Tristan was on his laptop booking a ticket as soon as he arrived home. He wasn't sure exactly what it was about Annika that had him hooked, but he knew from the moment he literally ran into her that he was attracted to her. He hadn't been seriously looking for someone to have a relationship with for quite a few years, but he always had a feeling he would know when the right woman came along. It felt right with Annika and the more time he spent with her, the more he fell in love with her. Oh heck, he was already madly in love with her and couldn't wait to see her again in a couple of days. It would be a surprise, though.

However, during the call that evening he asked for her parent's address, offering the excuse he wanted to send her something.

Annika felt glad to see her parents and relax after the whirlwind of events of the last few months. She happily filled her mother in on Tristan and how she was already in love with him.

Both her parents were excited to meet Tristan, although they weren't sure when it would be possible since they weren't planning on being in the Minneapolis area until spring, but they would find a way to make it happen.

Two days after she'd arrived in Phoenix, actually Scottsdale to be exact, she received a call from Tristan. "How's your day going?" he asked.

"Weather here is wonderful, how's it back in Minneapolis?"

"There were light flurries when my plane took off," he stated.

"Plane took off to where?"

"I've missed you. It's snowing in Minneapolis, so thought I'd spend a few days in the Phoenix area if you'd like some company?" Tristan asked.

"Really?" she asked.

"Yes, I'd love to meet your parents." Tristan laughed.

Annika could've sworn she'd heard his laugh close to the room where she stood. "Where are you?"

"Try opening the front door," he coaxed.

She ran to the door and flew into his arms, wildly kissing him.

"Man, a guy could get used to this," he said setting her back down on the doorstep.

"So, I take it this is Tristan," her dad stated, walking up to see what all the commotion was about.

"Glad to meet you, sir." Tristan shook his hand.

"Glad to meet you," her mother said smiling at him. "Please come in." She opened the door and they walked inside the house.

An hour later, Tristan and Annika left in what she assumed was his rental car to go to what she assumed was his hotel. *Who rents a Corvette?* "Where are we going," she asked as they entered an elite neighborhood in Scottsdale.

"It's a surprise," he said as he turned into a driveway.

"I'm confused," she said taking in the lavish landscaping and exquisite executive home.

He turned the car off. They got out and walked up to the front door. He opened the door and went inside.

She followed. "Whose house is this? Did you rent this as an Air B and B?" she asked.

"This is my house. One I'm hoping to share with you." He took her in his arms and spun them both around. "What do you think of it?"

"It's beautiful and I'd love to."

A few nights later on New Year's Eve, they enjoyed dinner at the Pinnacle Peak Golf Clubhouse with a couple of his friends who lived in Phoenix.

Close to midnight, they walked out onto the patio where the view of millions of stars were pristinely clear in the evening sky and the temperature was nowhere near freezing.

They stood wrapped in each other's arms, gazing up at the stars.

"I'm really glad I bumped into you that day," he whispered in her ear.

"Me, too. But, I think I bumped into you." She snuggled in closer to him.

"I love you, Annika." He kissed her as the crowd inside yelled and cheered Happy New Year.

"I love you, too," Annika whispered in his ear and kissed him.

She'd lost the bet with her friends. She'd lost her heart to Tristan. But ultimately, she'd won because she'd found Tristan who wanted the same things in life that she did.

Marriage and a family.

She knew now that they were meant for each other and New Year's Day was going to be the beginning of the best year ever.

Annika had a feeling their lives would always be filled with travel and adventures.

EPILOGUE

On New Year's Day, Annika pulled out her laptop and sent an email to her friends.

Josie, Alana, Ryley and Emma:

To all my Betting on Paris cohorts.
I have lost our bet, I am madly in love!

Can't wait to tell you all about Tristan and hope you can meet him soon.
All my love,
Annika.

ALMOND RICE PUDDING

A NORDIC CHRISTMAS TRADITION

Ingredients:

- 1 ½ Cups Rice
- 1 ½ Cups Milk
- ½ Cup Sugar
- 1 tsp Almond Flavoring
- 1 Cup Whipping Cream
- Sliced Almonds

Instructions:

Cook rice in a large saucepan, following directions. Stir in milk and sugar, heat slowly to boiling. Simmer for 25 minutes, stirring often until the milk is absorbed. Remove from heat. Stir in almond flavoring and cool. Beat whipping cream until stiff, then fold into rice. Place in a large bowl and mix in 1 whole almond. Serve warm and sprinkle with cinnamon sugar mixture.

Or chill and spoon raspberry sauce around the edge of the bowl before serving and garnish with sliced almonds. Makes 8 servings.

RASPBERRY SAUCE

- 2 packages of frozen raspberries
- 1 Tbsp. cornstarch

Thaw raspberries, drain syrup. In a small saucepan, mix syrup with cornstarch until sauce thickens slightly. Chill. Makes 1 ¾ cups.

ROSE MARIE MEUWISSEN
BIO

Rose Marie Meuwissen, a first-generation Norwegian American born and raised in Minnesota, always tries to incorporate her Norwegian heritage into her writing. After receiving a BA in Marketing from

Concordia University, a Masters in Creative Writing from Hamline University soon followed. Minnesota is still where she calls home.

She has traveled around the world, including Scandinavia, but still has many places to see, enjoys attending Scandinavian events, writing conferences and is usually busy writing Minnesota Lakes Contemporary Romances, Viking Time Travel Romances or Norwegian Traditions Children's Books.

Visit her at www.rosemariemeuwissen.com or www.realnorwegianseatlutefisk.com.

NOVELS:

- *Taking Chances*—a contemporary romance novel set in Minnesota and Arizona.
- *Married by Saturday*—a contemporary romance novel set in Minnesota and Montana.
- *Looking for Mr. Right*—a contemporary internet dating romance novel set on Prior Lake in Minnesota—*Coming soon!*

NOVELLAS:

- *Annika—A Christmas Romance*—a contemporary romance set in Minnesota with a Nordic theme during the Christmas Holidays.
- *Skol! Viking Blonde Ale*—a contemporary romance set in Minnesota at an Autumn festival complete with a fortune teller, ale and Vikings!
- *Choosing to Live*—a Norwegian woman's journey during WWII to survive the Nazi Occupation of Norway—*Coming soon!*

ANTHOLOGIES:

- *A Date for Valentine's Day*—a short romance set at Lafayette Country Club on Lake Minnetonka, Minnesota available in the anthology, **Romancing the Lakes of Minnesota—Valentine's Day.**
- *Dance of Love*—a short romance set at the Renaissance Fair in Shakopee, Minnesota, available in the anthology, *Festivals of Love.*
- *Dancing in the Moonlight*—a short romance set on Mille Lacs Lake, Minnesota available in the anthology, **Love in the Land of Lakes.**
- *A Kiss Under the Northern Lights*—a short romance set in Ely, Minnesota available in the anthology, **Northern Kisses.**

CHILDREN'S BOOKS—REAL NORWEGIAN'S SERIES:

- *Real Norwegians Eat Lutefisk*—a Children's book about the tradition of Lutefisk presented in both English and Norwegian.
- *Real Norwegians Eat Rømmegrøt*—the second Children's book in the series about the tradition of Rømmegrøt presented in both English and Norwegian.
- *Real Norwegians Eat Lefse*—the third Children's book in the series about the tradition of Lefse presented in both English and Norwegian.
- *Real Norwegians Eat Krumkake*—the fourth Children's book in the series about the tradition of Krumkake presented in both English and Norwegian—*Coming next!*

NOVELETTES—COMING SOON!

- *Hot Summer Nights*—a Summer romance set in Prior Lake, Minnesota on Prior Lake.
- *Railroad Ties*—an Autumn romance set in Two Harbors, Minnesota on Lake Superior.
- *Blizzard of Love*—a Winter romance set in Lutsen, Minnesota on Lake Superior.
- *Nor-Way to Love*—a Spring romance set in Minneapolis, Minnesota on Lake Harriet.
- *Old Yule Log Fires*—a Christmas romance set in Excelsior, Minnesota on Lake Minnetonka.

MICRO-MINI NOVELETTE—COMING SOON!

Christmas Notes—a collection of Christmas prose poems to warm the heart during the Christmas season.

AUTHOR'S NOTE

My Norwegian heritage is a large part of my everyday life which includes my membership in the Sons of Norway, Daughters of Norway, Lakselaget, and the Norway House in Minneapolis. My father was born in Norway and after enduring his teenage years under the Nazi Occupation of Norway during WWII, he came to the United States a year after the war ended. In Minnesota we are blessed to have an abundance of Norwegian events to attend and I wanted to share them with my readers. The *Almond Rice Pudding* Christmas tradition is always a part of my Christmas celebrations. I'm glad that I finally found a way to include these traditions in one of my romance stories. I hope you enjoy Annika and Tristan's Nordic Christmas adventure.

Rose Marie Meuwissen

PREVIEW COPYRIGHT INFORMATION

JOSIE—A CHRISTMAS ROMANCE
PREVIEW CHAPTER 1 BY BETH GILDERSLEEVE

Josie glanced at the clock above the front door and rolled her shoulders. Jamie should have been here by now. He was always here by this time on Friday afternoons. But today he'd had his six-month performance review at Haven Woodworks. What if it hadn't gone well? What if Jamie had gone directly to his old haunts and was now perched on a barstool? Should she call his sponsor? *Stop it!* She ordered herself. *He's just running late.* Josie grabbed the spray sanitizer and a rag to scrub the coffee shop's tables. Cleaning up other people's messes should settle her mind.

It didn't. Josie took her role as a bossy older sister to heart, and it was hard not to worry about Jamie. She and her twin, Josh, were ten years older than Jamie. They'd both ruled over Jamie growing up, but their coddling, protecting, and sibling over-lording hadn't been enough. During his senior year of high school, a new love had replaced Jamie's old loves of lacrosse and baseball —alcohol. Jamie was smart and clever, though. He'd hidden it from his parents, and he'd always been sober whenever Josie and Josh were home for the weekend.

It had been a several-year downward spiral for Jamie until the night he'd stumbled into oncoming traffic and had been struck by a car.

During rehab treatment, he'd tried to explain it to them. He felt like a puzzle piece from a different puzzle, like he just didn't fit with their family. Jamie's admission broke their hearts.

Over the course of a long and dreary winter, the Wright family rebuilt themselves. Jamie now felt like he fit in their family puzzle. He'd been sober for over a year, and he loved his job at Haven Woodworks. Josie would do everything in her power to keep it that way.

The bells above the front door jingled and Josie dropped her rag. She grinned as the woman, with an infant strapped to her chest and a preschooler in tow, approached and placed her order. "Go sit down and I'll bring your drinks to you," Josie said as she handed back the change. The woman smiled and nodded her head in agreement as she dumped her coins into the tip jar.

Josie kept an eye on the small family as she made their drinks. *Maybe someday*, she thought wistfully but then shook her head in disgust. *Who am I kidding? It's not going to happen*, she admitted. Even if she trusted her heart enough to give love another try, she didn't have the time or the energy to date. In her experience, men wanted attention. Josie didn't have any extra of that. Her eleven coffee shops required all of her energy and attention. She stopped her dreaming and carried the peppermint white chocolate mocha and the kiddie cocoa to the corner where they'd settled. The baby sat on her mother's lap and she smiled and giggled at Josie as she set the drinks on the table.

Too bad I can't have a family without a husband, Josie thought. Being a single-parent was an option for a lot of women, but she couldn't see herself going down that path. Until Mr. Right slipped into her life, Jo's Joe was her only baby.

Josie settled in behind the counter. She picked up the rag ready to resume cleaning when her eyes fell on her satchel. *Aw, crap!* she thought guiltily. She should look at the stack of reports instead of cleaning the already spotless bakery case, but she'd successfully ignored the reports all afternoon. A few more minutes wouldn't hurt.

She knew she wouldn't be able to concentrate on the endless rows and columns until she saw Jamie.

The front door opened and Josie looked up excitedly. It wasn't Jamie, but the high schoolers kept her busy making smoothies and warming up cookies. She'd just finished adding extra whipped cream to the top of the last strawberry smoothie when Jamie burst through the front door. If the sun had been out that day, Jamie's smile still would have outshone it.

Finally, Josie breathed a sigh of relief as she finished waiting on the teens. "How'd it go?" she asked him when he stepped up to the counter. She hoped her tone sounded casual. She didn't want Jamie to think she was being nosy or concerned. That had been one of his complaints during therapy. He'd argued that he had one mother, and he didn't need Josie mothering him, too. He wanted a sister. A comrade in arms. A partner in crime.

Jamie put his hands on the counter and leaned toward her. "Hey, how's your day been?" he asked, avoiding her question.

"No complaints. Do you want anything to drink?" Josie grabbed a nearby rag and wiped the espresso machine's gleaming steam wand. Jamie smirked. Josie's penchant for cleaning when she was worried was an ongoing joke in the family.

"Hmm. How about a medium, cherry, dark chocolate, mocha with extra whip and chocolate shavings?"

"Sounds like a celebration drink," Josie said, fishing for more information.

"Maybe," Jamie teased. Josie focused on tapping the espresso into the portafilter. *North, south, east, and west,* she thought as she pressed the tamper around the basket.

"Milk preference?" she asked. The only milk he didn't like was soy.

"Cow."

"Type?"

"Whole."

"Livin' large there, baby brother." She pulled the whole milk from the under-counter refrigerator.

"Seems appropriate for a celebration, though."

"Oh? Are we celebrating anything?" Josie played along as she poured the creamy milk into a clean steamer jug.

"Maybe," Jamie said. Josie relaxed her jaw and wished, and not for the first time, that Jamie was more communicative like Josh. But then again, she and Josh had that weird twin connection where they knew what the other one was thinking. Josie finished making the latte and turned back to Jamie. He'd pulled out his wallet.

"Put that back," she scolded. "You know it's on the house."

"Well, it's not every day I get a raise, so let me pay today, okay?" Josie heard the eagerness in his voice. *This is important to him*, she realized.

"Okay," Josie agreed and smiled as she rang up his order. As she did, he told her about his review. The only complaint the manager, Gabe Kane, had was that he couldn't clone Jamie. And if Jamie's next review went as well, they should talk about additional training, either in management or more skill-based woodworking, whichever Jamie preferred.

"But I'll do whatever Gabe wants me to," he said.

"Gabe's a smart man. He knows the best place for an employee is where their heart is. So don't agree to a management role to make him happy when your heart is in working with your hands. Gabe wouldn't appreciate it." Jamie nodded his head in agreement. Jamie worked with Gabe but Jo's Joe was Gabe's favorite caffeine fix. Josie saw him several times a week. Gabe was a good customer and friend. She glanced at the clock and her heart skipped a beat as she thought about Jamie's boss and her friend. *Just friend*, she reminded herself. *He should have been here by now, too*, she thought wistfully as she wiped a smudge off the bakery case.

"I think it's time I moved out," Jamie added before taking a sip of his latte. Josie took a deep breath before answering. This would be a big step for him. She knew it and so did he.

"This seems pretty sudden. Are you sure?"

"Actually, I've spoken to both Barry and Tim about this. Several times. They agree. I'm ready for this, and now, with the raise, I can afford something decent." Josie knew she should be happier for Jamie, especially since his counselor and AA sponsor were on board and supportive of his plans. But in many ways, she'd considered their cramped living arrangements since he'd left rehab to be her penance. If she'd been a more attentive sister, she could have kept him sober. Intellectually she knew that was crap, but emotionally she was tied to the idea tighter than a double knot.

"When?"

"I think Leesa and I will start looking this weekend."

"Oh, you're taking your girlfriend with you?" Jamie and Leesa had dated briefly in high school and had reconnected when Jamie had moved back to Haven after rehab.

"Unless you want to keep her and I'll take the TV?"

"Dream on." Josie rolled her eyes at him. "Take her. I need my bathroom space back. And a quiet night would be good for a change." Jamie blushed just as she'd known he would. "Congratulations, Jamie. I'm happy for you and proud of you. You worked hard for this."

"Thanks, Sis." They stared at each other, wearing identical goofy grins. He took another sip of his mocha and sported a slight whipped cream mustache. She didn't tell him. He'd figure it out soon enough, and it served him right for springing this move on her.

She wasn't the easygoing sibling, that was Josh. Josie had planned on Jamie living with her above her flagship store for at least another six months. "I'll see you later," he said and saluted her as he turned and walked out.

She reached for the slip of paper tucked into her apron. Her best friend since childhood, who was now her sister-in-law, had given her a daily calendar with mantras. Since both Elle and Josie were wound pretty tight, Josie hadn't taken it personally. She unfolded the slip and read today's reminder: "Let go or get dragged." *Easier said than done,* she thought as she stuffed the slip of paper back into her apron.

Josie looked up and frowned as the instigator of her current woes, Gabe Kane, manager and part-owner of Haven Woodworks, walked toward her. From the grey lacing his dark blond hair and the laugh lines around his light brown eyes, she'd put him in his early forties, but his body was that of a younger man, with broad shoulders and a narrow waist. That body had dated just about every single woman in Haven since he'd arrived last January. Except her. Josie didn't hold it against him. Not too much, at least.

She'd resigned herself to a life in singledom. There were worse fates, like a loveless marriage. She focused on that instead of the cloud of perpetual bliss that floated over Elle and Josh. Sure she'd love a husband, and children, but Josie had been burned by men: Michael, Silvano, and Jeff. *And just like in baseball, three strikes and I'm out*, she thought. For now, Josie was done with the game of love. She'd rather be safe and secure than risk it all hoping for a home run.

"Your usual?" she asked him, ignoring the way her heart sped up as it always did. Gabe Kane was an attractive man. She could look but she wouldn't touch.

Gabe nodded his head. "When I walked past the front window you were all smiles with Jamie, but I'm getting a frown. What's up?"

"You know how it is when you own a business. There's always something to worry about," she said as she started on his usual flat white.

"Tell me about it," he said. Josie shrugged her shoulders and returned her focus to the drink. "No, seriously. Tell me."

"I signed a contract with Hart Hotels to provide an exclusive signature blend of coffee for them."

"Doesn't sound like a problem to me."

"I'm not done yet, Mr. Impatient." Gabe didn't seem bothered by the reprimand. He just smiled at her in encouragement. "I need a new coffee roaster to handle the increased production. I've found the machine I want, we have the down payment, and Elle's arranged financing for the rest. We've even made plans for expedited shipping. But I haven't found a place for it. It's pretty big and I need a clean location that is nearby. There are lots of options twenty minutes away, but I'm not willing to compromise yet." She handed him his drink as several teens walked in.

"I've got a spot that would work," Gabe said as she handed him his drink.

"You do?"

"Yes. Come join me when you're done with them," he said, indicating the teens who had just rushed through the front door. She didn't appreciate the commanding tone in his voice, but if he had a solution for her, she'd overlook it. Plus, watching him walk away compensated for the tone. He settled into the farthest table. Josie kept an eye on Gabe as she dealt with the teens and their sugar-fueled drinks. He seemed off. Not his usual end-of-the-week vibe.

Josie poured herself a cup of decaf and plated a piece of pumpkin rum cake with maple cream cheese frosting for him. She was ready for a break and eager to learn more about the potential space. And to find out what was bugging him. She watched him as she approached but he didn't seem to notice. Josie focused her gaze out the large picture window to where he seemed to stare but all she saw was a gloomy November afternoon. Nothing special and nothing unusual at this time of the year. A few dry leaves chased down the sidewalk. The snow hadn't yet fallen in Haven, so there was nothing to impede their race. She set her coffee and the cake down on the table. He startled. "Are you sure you want company?" she asked.

"Only if it's you." He motioned toward the seat across from him.

"You'd think after five years my body would be used to this," Josie said as she sat down. She sighed happily.

"You get up too early and you don't delegate enough."

"Takes one to know one," she retorted.

"Touché." She saw Gabe eye the cake. "What's this?"

"A piece of cake. For you. You look like you could use something sweet." She pushed it toward him.

"Better get yourself a fork so you can help me eat this. I had a late lunch and there's no way I'm finishing this." Josie pulled a fork out of her apron and grinned. "That's my girl," he said and winked at her before his pensive mood settled back around him. Gabe ate from the bottom of the cake and Josie focused on the top. She paced herself. One bite for her for every two bites of his. While he may have had a late lunch, she hadn't had any. She was hungry and this was a superb cake, if she did say so herself.

They ate in comfortable silence, the kind you have with a good friend. And Gabe was a good friend, she realized. They'd become close since he'd moved to Haven almost a year ago. He'd spent his time revitalizing Haven Woodworks. The company manufactured kitchen cabinets and interior doors, the types carried at big-box home improvement stores. He'd also started a new line that focused on custom-made cabinets and front doors, and that was the line Jamie worked on. Jamie had mentioned a rumor of adding a line of furniture, too, but Gabe had said nothing to her about it, so she'd discounted the rumor.

Gabe's focus on the plant and expanding production had meant an increase in good jobs. He'd made an effort to hire people who were getting back on their feet after drug and alcohol rehabilitation programs, like Jamie. Haven Woodworks even sponsored an AA meeting at the plant every day. It was in a back room that had its own entrance from the parking lot. Jamie said she'd be shocked if she knew how many downtown workers attended the meetings, too.

It wasn't unusual for Josie and Gabe to bounce business ideas off each other. Several times, Elle, in her capacity as CEO of Jo's Joe, and Josh, as her director of marketing, had joined them and the four of them had tackled problems for the coffee shops and Woodworks. Most of the coffee shop problems had focused on how Josie could effectively and efficiently continue to grow the business. She now had eleven shops in the area surrounding Haven and the eastern suburbs of St. Paul. In the several years that Elle had been with her, they'd added six stores, but they wanted to ramp that number up to three a year.

After the second time the four of them met, Josh had teased Josie that she should move her and Gabe's daily coffee dates out into the real world to see if it worked there, too. But Josie liked it the way it was. She was comfortable with Gabe and comfortable with her life for the most part.

Maybe someday she'd trust herself enough with men to come out of her self-imposed shell and play the dating game again. Josie wasn't a naive girl anymore, and she'd learned a lot about men since being duped thrice.

Her innocence about men had first been battered by Michael. After high school, she'd had no idea what she wanted to do, so she decided not to go to college right away. She had always been interested in food and baking so her father had suggested she move out to San Francisco to work for her aunt, who owned an upscale restaurant there, and learn as much as she could.

Her aunt was a generous soul but a hard taskmaster. No favoritism for Josie. She'd started by washing dishes and worked her way up the kitchen food chain. It hadn't taken long for the sous chef, Michael, to notice her.

Michael was handsome and sophisticated. At ten years her senior, he was a worldwide traveler with exotic tales to tell. It hadn't taken long for her to fall under his spell and for Michael to take her under his wing. That he'd also seen a naive girl eager to please had escaped her.

She'd fallen hard and fast for him. It had been exciting and fairly innocent. Long looks. Heated glances. Passionate kisses. The hostess and the head bartender had tried to warn her, but she'd put it down to jealousy.

Michael had insisted they keep their relationship as quiet as possible; he didn't want to lose his job. The secrecy had only added fuel to her desire. She'd thought she'd loved him and that he'd felt the same. Who knew? Maybe he had.

They'd talked and planned about where to open their own restaurant and what they'd serve their eager diners. They'd poured over each other's personal recipes. They'd dreamed and they'd plotted, but he'd never mentioned his wife. Or his toddler. Josie had been devastated when she'd learned the truth. Even now her stomach turned when she thought about being the other woman. About being played.

Michael had admitted that he'd hoped Josie could influence her aunt to promote him to head chef at the restaurant she was opening across the bay. Josie knew she couldn't work with him any longer, and as much as she wanted to complain to her aunt and see him fired, she couldn't do it. He had a family to support and she only had to support herself.

So she'd fabricated a story for her aunt about wanting to learn about desserts and maybe train to be a pastry chef. It hadn't been a total lie. At that time Josie had been very focused on desserts and ice cream, and she had the ten-pound post-breakup weight gain to prove it.

As luck would have it, her aunt had a friend who owned several coffee shops in the Bay Area that were known for both their coffee and their desserts. Once again Josie started at the bottom and worked her way up. A year later, she was an excellent but uncertified pastry chef, and she'd found her passion—coffee.

Her boss had connections to a coffee plantation in Costa Rica, and she had been more than happy to arrange an internship for Josie.

Josie had worked side by side with Silvano, the plantation owner's son. He'd taught her everything he knew about growing and harvesting coffee beans and the science of roasting and brewing. After several months, she'd started to trust him, and she gave in to his insistent offers of sightseeing and dinners. Josie knew he couldn't use her because she had no skills or connections of value to him.

Their romance had bloomed. They'd talked about marriage and buying their own land and how Silvano would do things differently than his father did. He'd modernize and help their growers by providing better pay and benefits. By the time she'd realized that Silvano was a dreamer and a schemer, it had been too late; her heart was already invested.

She'd overheard him bragging to a buddy that he'd soon be exchanging a diamond engagement ring for a green card. As soon as that happened, he'd be moving to the States and leaving the miserable plantation behind him. His soon-to-be-fiancée was smart and a hard worker. He didn't think she'd have any problem providing for the two of them.

Josie had never packed so quickly in her life. She'd caught the next plane out and headed back to Minnesota. She was done with men. They were liars and cheats, and she obviously didn't have enough common sense to tell the good ones from the bad. For her own protection, no more relationships. Not until she trusted herself or had the funds to run thorough background checks.

While she'd waited for the fall semester to start at the University of Minnesota's food science program, she'd returned to her high school job, serving customers and making coffee drinks at Haven's only non-chain coffee shop. The irony wasn't lost on her or her family. After all her travels, she was right back where she'd started.

Maybe when I'm done with that silly Paris bet, I'll try one of the dating apps, Josie thought as she sipped her coffee. While on her annual girls' vacation with her college roommates, they'd all agreed to focus on their goals and not on men. They'd called it the Paris Bet. Josie rolled her eyes at the memory and then looked down at the cake for her next bite. Gabe had eaten the bottom layer and had tunneled the cake out from the next layer. "You don't like frosting?" she asked. She was suspicious of anyone who claimed they didn't like sugar. It was unnatural.

"Not as much as you seem to," Gabe teased.

"To be honest, I don't think anyone likes frosting as much as I do. It's the perfect combination of sugar and fat. Just like us," she proclaimed before scooping up another forkful.

"Are you calling me fat?" Gabe asked in mock indignation. "Because no one has ever called me sweet."

"No." Josie laughed and shook her head. "Just my lame attempt at making a comparison. We're like coffee and cream, peanut butter and jelly, coffee and chocolate."

"I sense a theme here," Gabe said and Josie saw the teasing glint in his eyes. She blundered on before she could stop herself. "You're a good friend, Gabe, and you've helped Jamie a lot. My whole family is indebted to you. I know hiring him was a risk, so I'm glad it's seemed to work out well for both of you."

"It has worked out well. Jamie's a great kid and a hard worker."

"I don't think my baby brother would appreciate his boss calling him a kid."

"I know. But when I'm staring down the barrel of thirty-seven, he seems like a kid. If I only knew then what I know now," he added sadly.

"Sounds like you've got a heap of regrets and a birthday coming up. When?"

"This Sunday." Gabe set his fork down and pushed the plate toward Josie. He slumped down in the wooden chair and crossed his arms over his broad chest as he turned his head toward the window. Josie couldn't help but notice his clenched, chiseled jaw.

"I'll get us refills and then you can tell me, okay?" Josie stood and gathered their empty mugs. Concern for Gabe had wiped out her curiosity about the potential roasting space. Gabe turned his head back toward her.

"You might not like what I have to say." His words sounded like a warning.

"I'll take my chances," Josie said over her shoulder as she walked back to the barista station.

Made in the USA
Monee, IL
03 November 2023

45738513R00106